7 BILLION LIVES ARE IN DANGER.
13 STRANGERS WITH TERRIFYING NIGHTMARES.
1 ENEMY WILL STOP AT NOTHING TO DESTROY US ALL.

MY NAME IS SAM.
I AM ONE OF THE LAST THIRTEEN.
OUR BATTLE CONTINUES . . .

This one is for Raff, who I owe her weight in chocolate—JP.

First American Edition 2014
Kane Miller, A Division of EDC Publishing

Text copyright © James Phelan, 2014
Illustrations & design copyright © Scholastic Australia, 2014
Illustrations by Chad Mitchell. Design by Nicole Stofberg

First published by Scholastic Australia Pty Limited in 2014
This edition published under license from Scholastic Australia Pty Limited.

Cover photography: Blueprint © istockphoto.com/Adam Korzekwa; Parkour Tic-Tac © istockphoto.com/Willie B. Thomas; Climbing wall © istockphoto.com/microgen; Leonardo da Vinci (Sepia) © istockphoto.com/pictore; Gears © istockphoto.com/-Oxford-; Mechanical blueprint © istockphoto.com/teekid; Circuit board © istockphoto.com/Bjorn Meyer; Map © istockphoto.com/alengo; Grunge drawing © istockphoto.com/aleksandar velasevic; World map © istockphoto.com/Maksim Pasko; Internet © istockphoto.com/Andrey Prokhorov; Inside clock © istockphoto.com/LdF; Space galaxy © istockphoto.com/Sergii Tsololo; Sunset © istockphoto.com/Joakim Leroy; Blue flare © istockphoto.com/YouraPechkin; Global communication © istockphoto.com/chadive samanthakamani; Earth satellites © istockphoto.com/Alexey Popov; Girl portrait © istockphoto.com/peter zelei; Student & board © istockphoto.com/zhang bo; Young man serious © istockphoto.com/Jacob Wackerhausen; Portrait man © istockphoto.com/Alina Solovyova-Vincent; Sad expression © istockphoto.com/Shelly Perry; Content man © istockphoto.com/drbimages; Pensive man © istockphoto.com/Chuck Schmidt; Black and pink © istockphoto.com/blackwaterimages; Punk Girl © istockphoto.com/Kuzma; Woman escaping © Jose antonio Sanchez reyes/Photos.com; Young running man © Tatiana Belova/Photos.com; Gears clock © Jupiterimages/Photos.com; Young woman © Anomen/Photos.com; Explosions © Leigh Prather | Dreamstime.com; Landscape blueprints © Firebrandphotography | Dreamstime.com; Jump over wall © Ammentorp | Dreamstime.com; Mountains, CAN © Akadiusz Iwanicki | Dreamstime.com; Sphinx Bucegi © Adrian Nicolae | Dreamstime.com; Big mountains © Hoptrop | Dreamstime.com; Sunset mountains © Pklimenko | Dreamstime.com; Mountains lake © Janmika | Dreamstime.com; Blue night sky © Mack2happy | Dreamstime.com; Old writing © Empire331 | Dreamstime.com; Young man © Shuen Ho Wang | Dreamstime.com; Abstract cells © Sur | Dreamstime.com; Helicopter © Evren Kalinbacak | Dreamstime.com; Aeroplane © Rgbe | Dreamstime.com; Phrenology illustration © Mcarrel | Dreamstime.com; Abstract interior © Sur | Dreamstime.com; Papyrus © Cebreros | Dreamstime.com; Blue shades © Mohamed Osama | Dreamstime.com; Blue background © Matusciac | Dreamstime.com; Sphinx and Pyramid © Dan Breckwoldt | Dreamstime.com; Blue background2 © Cammeraydave | Dreamstime.com; Abstract shapes © Lisa Mckown | Dreamstime.com; Yellow Field © Simon Greig | Dreamstime.com; Blue background3 © Sergey Skrebnev | Dreamstime.com; Blue eye © Richard Thomas | Dreamstime.com; Abstract landscape © Crazy80frog | Dreamstime.com; Rameses II © Jose I. Soto | Dreamstime.com; Helicopter © Sculpies | Dreamstime.com; Vitruvian man © Cornelius20 | Dreamstime.com; Scarab beetle © Charon | Dreamstime.com; Eye of Horus © Charon | Dreamstime.com; Handsome male portrait © DigitalHand Studio/Shutterstock.com; Teen girl © CREATISTA/Shutterstock.com; Somewhere © istockphoto.com/TimothyBall; Australian landscape © istockphoto.com/sara_winter; Left turn in the Outback © Oskarwells | Dreamstime.com; Devils Marbles outback Australia granite boulders © Dirk Ercken | Dreamstime.com; Red track in the Outback © Csld | Dreamstime.com; Australian Outback Eucalyptus and Outbuildings © Travelling-light | Dreamstime.com; Wild nature in the Australian Outback © Ladiras81 | Dreamstime.com; Off road car on rough road © Uros Ravbar | Dreamstime.com; Sydney © Steve Mann | Dreamstime.com; Sydney © Warren Gibb | Dreamstime.com; Sydney skyline © Andrew Chambers | Dreamstime.com; Sydney skyline © Cenk Unver | Dreamstime.com; Sydney © Explorer Media Pty Ltd Sport The Library | Dreamstime.com; Captain Cook's ship © Ben Mcleish | Dreamstime.com; Night of Christchurch © Liwen Zhang | Dreamstime.com; Christchurch Art Gallery © Matthew Weinel | Dreamstime.com; Christchurch city scene © Intodune | Dreamstime.com; Christchurch city scene © Intodune | Dreamstime.com; Christchurch gondola top station © Serget | Dreamstime.com; Captain Cook © istockphoto.com/GeorgiosArt; Ancient map and compass © istockphoto.com/travellinglight; Pitcairn Island in the South Pacific © istockphoto.com/kensorrie; Historic Anasazi petroglyphs © istockphoto.com/Pi-Lens; Petroglyph of man © istockphoto.com/Lokibaho; Changing colors of Uluru © Matthew Weinel | Dreamstime.com; Uluru © Mazzel1986 | Dreamstime.com.
Internal photography: p125, Vault door © istockphoto.com | cscredon.

For information contact:
Kane Miller, A Division of EDC Publishing
PO Box 470663
Tulsa, OK 74147-0663
www.kanemiller.com
www.edcpub.com
www.usbornebooksandmore.com

Library of Congress Control Number: 2013945970

Printed and bound in the United States of America
1 2 3 4 5 6 7 8 9 10
ISBN: 978-1-61067-281-8

THE LAST THIRTEEN

BOOK ELEVEN

JAMES PHELAN

Kane Miller
A DIVISION OF EDC PUBLISHING

PREVIOUSLY

Just as he begins to lose hope, Sam is rescued at sea. Befriended by the Japanese Prime Minister, and with help from Issey's grandfather, Sam and Tobias leave for Cambodia, where Sam has dreamed he will meet the next of the last 13.

At the Academy, Eva discovers that a Doors team has been sabotaged but the competition will go on. Traveling to Istanbul, Eva, Xavier and Zara prepare to face their fears and enter the dream construct.

On their way to Angkor Wat, Sam and Tobias are ambushed by local bandits. Tobias' quick thinking saves them and they continue to the temple where they meet Poh, the next Dreamer. He is ready for Sam and revisits his dream to find his Gear.

Alex decides to stay on Hans' super yacht, playing along with him to discover his plans. They sail south but are attacked by drone planes sent by Stella. Fending them off, they arrive at the Marshall Islands where they are taken hostage by local pirates.

Tobias remains on guard while Sam and Poh navigate an amazing complex of tunnels under Angkor Wat. Poh finds his Gear around the neck of an incredible elephant statue and inadvertently sets off a trap, filling the chamber with water.

Meanwhile, Eva, Xavier and Zara enter the Doors construct where Eva quickly discovers something is amiss. Searching for the others, she is attacked by Solaris. With great courage, Eva faces her worst fear and escapes the Doors. She awakens to find Xavier has been "lost" inside the construct and is fighting for his life.

Poh leads Sam to safety but when they return to their camp, Tobias is missing. Sam finds him wounded in the forest, attacked once more by the bandits. He is badly injured and dies in Sam's arms.

Heavyhearted, Sam travels to New York where the Japanese Prime Minister has arranged for Sam to speak to the UN. Putting on a brave face, Sam stands before the General Assembly and reveals the existence of Dreamers, the prophecy and that they only have fourteen days left to save the world . . .

EVA'S NIGHTMARE

"**R**un, Eva! Run!"

I hear Sam's voice but I cannot find him among the hundreds of faces passing by me.

"Eva!" Sam yells again.

His voice sounds distant and I can't place where it's coming from in the busy plaza.

"Eva—up *here!*"

I look up from where I stand, shielding my eyes from the bright sun.

Sam is a tiny speck above me, standing on top of one of the most recognizable buildings in the world—the Sydney Opera House. Its huge white sails seem to sparkle in the sunlight, the dappled reflections of the nearby water making the glimmering walls look like they're moving.

What is he doing up there?

"Sam!" I call out. "How'd you—"

"Behind you!" Sam shouts, pointing way over my head. "You have to run!"

I turn.

There's a commotion in the crowd. Voices cry out and

the crowd begins to disperse, running. They're scattering in all directions–*away* from something.

Or, rather, *someone* . . .

A black-clad figure blasts through the masses and is headed straight for me.

Solaris.

Oh no . . .

No sooner have I spotted him than a blaze of fire streams over my head.

I turn and run. It's hard to break through the crowd of startled and screaming tourists. I am knocked to the ground in the stampede, but quickly get back to my feet and run up the wide stairs. I glance over my shoulder. Solaris is following, slowly and purposefully, yet somehow he's gaining on me. I run towards the doors, trying to conjure up thoughts of something safe that might be beyond them— Lora with a team of Guardians, armed and ready, or Sam, there to lead us to a secret exit where a helicopter waits . . .

The thought stops me in my tracks.

Fire flashes again. My vision burns, blinding me, the ground beneath me circles, spinning fast.

But how . . . ?

The screaming crowds, the tall buildings, the bustling city have disappeared. I look out into an expansive sky—the colors of the light have changed. Even the air feels different. And now I'm flying aboard a helicopter.

I'm in a dream. I did this . . . I made this happen.

I breathe in deeply, trying to not let the fear of being so high up overcome me. I turn to look at the pilot next to me. He's big and strong, with long dark hair and dark skin. I don't recognize him but I think that he must be a Guardian, though he's not wearing the usual uniform. I notice a long scar zigzagging up his left arm. He sees me looking at him and points down at the ground.

Reluctantly, I turn to look where he's pointing, trying to look outward, not downward.

Outside it seems like a different kind of bright. The sun is still on top of us, but the sky is a deeper blue and the ground below is burned orange and dusty. Everything seems so endless.

My eyes focus on something tiny, far in the distance.

As we near, I realize there is someone there. He is waving his arms over his head, signaling desperately to get our attention as we approach.

Someone with short dark hair and glasses.

We hover over this boy and I gasp in shock as I suddenly understand.

It's Sam.

Why is he wearing glasses? And what happened to his hair? What's going on?

"Hold on!" says the pilot, as the helicopter banks sharply and circles around. "I'll find a spot to land!"

I give him a shaky thumbs-up, my other hand beside me clinging tightly to the edge of the seat. I feel my heart rate accelerate as we go through the maneuver, my head spinning as the ground twirls closer in the helicopter's ever tighter turns. I see Sam again as we pivot around, still waving at us. At first I think he's smiling, but as I get a longer look, I see his mouth is moving. He's saying something—no, *shouting* something.

I feel a cold shiver run down my spine.

Sam's not waving at us.

He's warning us.

I look out the window, twisting my body to see further back. There's another aircraft out there in the sky, another helicopter. It's painted in military greens and browns, with its side doors open. I can see it's loaded with weapons— missiles and heavy machine guns.

I've seen a helicopter like this before . . . in the Alps.

There's a bright flash and a plume of smoke streaks across the brilliant blue sky. The missile heads in a straight line towards us.

I've seen this before too.

There seems little hope of escape. I know how this ends.

But it's my dream . . . control it, Eva. You're not ready to wake up, you have to see the rest of this dream. Think.

I close my eyes, feeling calm despite what is coming. I will myself to change my surroundings, to be somewhere else.

The world spins and I feel weightless, as though floating on a sea.

"Eva, wake up!"

I open my eyes.

Sam is next to me. He's still wearing the thick, black-framed glasses. One of the lenses is cracked and his hair is as black as mine. He's running next to me. It's dark and our path is lit only by Sam's flashlight.

I'm moving as fast as Sam is, but I frown in confusion because I know I'm not running.

I look around in the darkness and am startled to realize the helicopter pilot is carrying me, cradled in his arms like a small child, as he runs alongside Sam.

"What . . . happened?" I ask.

"The helicopter went down, a missile, just like before," Sam says. "No backyard pool to splash down in this time, though."

"Then how did we . . .?" My mind is blank. I try to shake the confusion clear but I still can't recall. I lean upward a little to look behind us and can see the glow of a large fire.

"We have to get out of here," Sam says. "They're after us. Can you run?"

"I—yes—I don't know . . ."

It feels as though my arms and legs are not mine. I try to move them but I can't.

"What happened?" I ask again. It's night now and there are more stars in the sky than I have ever seen.

"We have to get out of here," Sam repeats.

"Where are we?" I ask. I look around the horizon. There's nothing to see, nothing but . . .

What is that?

Something ahead glows in the darkness, illuminated by powerful spotlights. Huge white structures, like golf balls. It looks like a space station, like I'm on the moon or another planet or something.

"Why are we running?" I say to Sam.

"Because of what you've got!" Sam says, pointing at me.

I'm confused, starting to get frustrated with Sam's evasive answers, but I look down. Hanging on my dream catcher necklace is a shiny object. Even in the dim light I know immediately what it is.

A Gear.

It's unlike any that I have seen before in the race.

"How'd I get this?" I ask.

"We were hoping you could tell us," Sam says.

"Where are we?" I ask.

"Australia," the Guardian carrying me says as he runs after Sam. "We're in Australia."

"Wait . . ." I say, and to my surprise, the two of them stop running, obedient. "Sam?"

"Yes."

"We're in *my* dream," I say, wriggling out of the Guardian's hold and dropping to the ground to stand on my own two feet. *"I've* got this."

I turn around and, clutching the Gear, I close my eyes to concentrate.

Go back, Eva. See it all. From the start. How'd you get here? Where'd you find this Gear? See it all. Every step, so that you will know where to go in the waking world. You can do this . . . control it.

I open my eyes.

Daylight.

"Yes!"

I'm back in Sydney.

But my elation is short-lived, replaced instead by panic when I realize that this time, *I'm* on top of the Opera House, way, way up high. I crouch down and my arms fling out to hold on to something–*anything*–to steady myself. The height makes my head spin and my heart race. The strong wind buffeting me makes the terrifying distance from the ground worse. I start to breathe, fast and furious, but then hold my breath completely at the sound of something familiar.

"You're getting good at this, Eva . . ." It is Solaris' voice, amplified and menacing. "But no matter how far or how fast you run in your dreams, I will always be there. You will *never* outrun me."

He charges at me, becoming a shapeless black blur. The full force of his momentum knocks me over the edge. I see him standing there above me as I fall into—

Nothingness.

ALEX

The sea was calm and quiet. The pirates, on the other hand, were not.

How is it even possible to make that much noise when you're asleep?

The snores and snuffling noises coming from the main living area was the good news, as Alex could easily tell where the pirates were on the *Ra*. The bad news was that even though they seemed a little carefree with security, overconfident about their superior numbers and weaponry, they were not dumb enough to completely forget about leaving a night watch. That guy was walking around, looking out for trouble.

Great.

Locked up in Hans' stateroom with the others, Alex was the only one small or agile enough to fit through the port window. He'd gotten to this point quickly and without any trouble. The next part would be tougher.

But Alex had an escape plan and was determined to see it through. He clung to the outside of the *Ra's* hull, holding on to the rail, his back arched and his feet shuffling along.

His toes were balanced shakily on a ridge along the hull's side. Even at this hour of the night, the pirates had the boat going at quite a speed, slicing through the dark Pacific waters.

The guy on night watch was smoking. Alex could smell it on the breeze.

"Disgusting habit," Alex murmured under his breath, positioning himself below the guard, clinging on to the handrail and the side of the boat. The pirate's machine gun was strapped around his back. Alex extended up onto his toes, lifting himself up closer and closer to the back of the guard . . .

He grabbed the barrel of the gun and pulled, *hard*.

The pirate flipped backward over the bow of the super yacht, disappearing into the deep black sea with the smallest of splashes.

"Shoulda quit while you had the chance, buddy," Alex muttered, wincing at the desperate cries of the pirate as they sailed away from him.

Alex still had the guy's machine gun in his hand.

This should come in handy.

"That was easy . . ." he said to himself, getting up onto the forward deck, carefully and quietly making his way to the bridge, gun at the ready. He ducked down under the windows to consider his position.

Now what—shoot my way out? No way.

OK, think. They're just pirates, making the most of the fact that the world's gone crazy to expand their criminal activities.

But . . . what if they know me? What if they're here because they think I'm one of the last 13? Or maybe this is just a setup, Hans could be in on it . . . but that doesn't make sense, I've been with him all this time.

Alex's spiraling thoughts were disrupted by a voice coming from the bridge.

Are there two more of them up there? Or is the pilot on the radio?

Alex stayed where he was, trying to figure out what he was up against, when suddenly the door next to him burst open.

SAM

Sam moved fast, seamlessly stitching together a jujitsu block and throw, putting his instructor down to the mat and then locking her into a compliance hold.

"Yield," the instructor said. "I yield."

Sam released the pressure on her shoulder and elbow lock and backed away. He put a towel around his neck and wiped away the sweat beading his forehead. He shook hands with his instructor and sat down at the side of the dojo to catch his breath.

As he had done again and again over these last few days, he made his mind think back to his address at the UN. He could still feel the stares of the Assembly when he spoke. Still picture the cameras with their red lights flashing, all focused on him. He had felt calm as he explained about the race and of the thirteen special teenagers who would lead it. But as he recalled the end of his speech, he could still hear the desperation in his voice as he asked for help.

The world's reaction had been swift and unexpected. The race, and those within it, were now global news.

"That was intense," a voice said. Sam's head snapped up

and he saw Eva standing in the doorway.

Sam remained silent. He got up and walked past her, out of the gymnasium and across the great lawn of the Academy's London campus, through an avenue of elm trees, their bare branches pointing starkly up into the winter sky. Eva followed close behind. Students were starting to pour out of the main building, their school day over. It was a world from which Sam was feeling more and more distant.

"Sam, we have to talk," Eva said.

"No, we don't."

"My dream—"

"No."

"I had it. *The* dream—the one that makes me one of the last 13."

Sam stopped and looked long and hard at her without speaking.

I knew this was coming but I still can't work out if I'm happy or not. More people I care about in more danger . . . but she's super smart and brave. Maybe braver than me.

"Sam?" Eva said. "Come back to me from wherever you are. I need you now, more than ever. I finally see where I fit in and that's amazing—and the scariest thing in the world. I *know* you understand." She reached out for him. "Nothing? You've nothing to say to me now?"

Sam hesitated for a moment, then kept walking.

"OK, never mind that *I* need you. We *all* do. And it's not good for you to shut down like this." Eva sighed, worried. "We've barely seen you, since the funeral, I mean . . ."

Sam said nothing, staring straight ahead, his expression blank.

"I know how you must be feeling, Sam, but you should talk about it. We all miss Tobias, you know."

Sam stopped mid-stride, flinching at the sound of Tobias' name. "Yeah? You think you know how this feels? Well, you didn't *see* him, you weren't there. You didn't see him take his last breath. Or hear his last words . . ." Sam stopped himself, shocked to find himself shouting.

Eva's eyes widened, filling with tears. "I'm sorry, Sam. I'm so sorry . . . I didn't mean . . . I don't know what else to say."

Sam looked at Eva, his closest friend. He immediately regretted his outburst—wished he'd stayed silent and blocked the grief from surfacing as he'd done up to now.

None of this is her fault.

"There's nothing *to* say," he said quietly. "There's nothing anyone can say that will bring him back or make any of this less terrible."

Sam started walking towards the dorm building again. He reached his room, going inside, but leaving the door open behind him. Eva followed and sat on the floor at the end of his bed.

Sam stared absently out the window, his back to Eva.

"The others want to see you too," she said. "After nearly losing Xavier in Istanbul . . ."

"I was there, you know," Sam said. "Not at the Doors, but—"

"Sam, please, it's OK if you don't want to talk."

"No, I mean . . . your dream. I know that I have to go to Australia with you."

Eva looked up, shocked. "You dreamed it too?"

Sam nodded. "It's dangerous out there, Eva. Like, *really* dangerous."

"I know that."

"Do you?"

"Yes, of course I do." Sam turned to look at Eva and could see the expression on her face slowly change as she understood what he was saying. "You think I shouldn't go with you."

"You could die out there," he said. "He—Tobias—knew the dangers better than anyone. And even he couldn't stop what was coming for him."

"Oh, Sam . . ." Eva stood up and came over to give Sam a hug.

"It's changed how I see everything," Sam said, unresponsive. "He was more than just a teacher to me. He was like a best friend, someone I could trust, someone I could go to if I needed . . . and now he's gone. He wasn't even killed by Solaris, but some random violence we never even saw coming. I don't know why that makes it worse, but it does. I know that's crazy."

"It's not crazy, I can understand why you'd say that," Eva said. "I'm sorry, Sam, I really am."

"No, it's not understandable, no one understands," he said.

Outside in the fading light of the afternoon, some students were starting hockey practice against a neighboring school. Sam watched them running over the field. "Look at them down there. It's like they don't have a care in the world . . ."

"It's not that, Sam," Eva said. "Life goes on for them, no matter what. That's a good thing. They feel safe and secure, because of you. Do you realize that? They believe in you—that you can win this for them. Sam, I don't think we need a superhero to save us. I think all we need is a regular guy. And maybe a few of his friends . . . we *need* you, Sam."

Sam let out a tired sigh.

"What do you think Tobias would want us to do?" Eva wondered. He could feel Eva looking at him, waiting for an answer.

"I know . . . I know." Sam sighed again. "I'm just tired of all this. Tired of running, of fighting. Tired of being the one that everyone is counting on to do a good job. Tired of losing people . . ."

Eva put an arm around his shoulders, the two of them looking out the window, beyond the sports field. "You know the name the media have given this place?" she said, motioning to where white tanks and helicopters from the UN circled the perimeter of the campus.

"The nightmare zone," Sam said.

"Yep. The nightmare zone." The two of them laughed. "It's like something out of a really bad movie, our new little city state they've created around the school grounds. Their soldiers watching our every move while they debate what to do. 'No one in or out without UN chaperones.' Talk about crazy!"

"Yeah, except it's not a movie. Not exactly what I was expecting either," Sam said, resigned.

"After *your* speech?" Eva asked. "What were you expecting?"

"I don't know. Tobias thought we could . . . well, I don't

know, but I don't think they truly get what's going on."

"Hmm. But we have to go out there. You and me," Eva said. "You *know* that, don't you? We have to follow my—*our*—dream. It's our destiny to get the next Gear."

Sam looked at her. "I always knew your time would come, Eva," he said.

Eva laughed nervously. "All this time, wondering if I would be one of the 13, but kind of knowing all along. Now that I have the responsibility, I hope I'm up to it."

"I believe you are. And I'm so glad you've had your dream now."

"So does that mean you're ready for our next adventure?" she said, a slow smile coming back to her face.

ALEX

The pirate crashed out the door, his forward momentum carrying him straight towards the railing ahead. In a lucky moment of timing, Alex was there to give him a little helping hand and he went overboard in one swift movement. The splash was a lot louder this time and the pirate's startled scream echoed in the night, even over the engine's noise. Alex held his breath, expecting trouble at any moment.

"And stay out!" someone yelled out the door. "Do not come back!"

Can't believe they didn't hear that.

He crept closer to the open doorway and listened.

Now there was only silence. He stole a glance around the doorway. A huge pirate stood at the wheel.

Alex gripped the old machine gun tighter.

Sneak in, club him and knock him out. OK.

On three.

One.

Two.

Two and a half . . .

Alex let out the big breath that he'd been holding and barreled through the door, half expecting to see the pirate waiting for him. But the man was still standing at the wheel, his broad back to Alex.

WHACK!

The guy slumped to the ground as Alex used the butt of the gun to club the pirate on the side of his beefy head.

"Two for two," Alex said, a small smile on his face. "Not bad batting—"

He paused as he smelled something vile, like decaying fish and ripe blue cheese . . . he jumped as he felt a heavy hand on his shoulder.

Alex turned around slowly. "Oh boy."

He recognized this pirate. He was a huge guy, easily the biggest of the twelve pirates he had counted earlier. He had long straggly hair, a tanned and craggy face, a huge grin revealing missing teeth. The few teeth that remained were like lonely black tombstones, rotting in his swollen gums.

Gross.

"You know," Alex said, trying to buy time and figure out what to do, the machine gun still in his hands as he took a step back, "maybe with your loot or bounty or whatever it is you pirates call all the stuff that you steal, maybe spend a little of it at the dentist? Or buy a toothbrush? Mouthwash or floss even. They say you should only floss the teeth that you want to keep . . ."

The giant bared his teeth in an angry grimace, a low

snarl sounding from the back of his throat.

OK, maybe the wrong approach.

In a fleeting second of inspiration, Alex suddenly looked wide-eyed and terrified over the pirate's shoulder. The guy fell for it and instinctively turned to check behind him, dropping his guard for a split second.

Alex pounced. He swung the gun, arcing it high through the air with his weight behind it.

CLONK!

It hit the pirate's head and the reverberation from the impact traveled back through the gun, down Alex's arms and right through his body, rattling Alex's own teeth in the process.

The giant pirate did not budge. He stared at Alex, his snarl even louder now.

Oh man!

The pirate pulled out a knife. It was a big rusty blade with a dull gleam to it.

Alex fumbled to turn the gun around in his hands.

The pirate took a step closer.

So maybe he knows I'm not about to shoot anyone.

Alex extended his other hand. "Look, maybe we just got off on the wrong foot. Hi, I'm Alex."

"Arghh!" the pirate lunged for Alex. Alex ducked the attack and scurried around the giant, out the open door behind him. He turned right, hugging the bridge wall, waiting. The giant pirate came rushing out.

Alex kicked out a leg, tripping him.

The pirate hit the handrail hard, which barely reached above the height of his knees.

"Arghh!"

SPLASH!

Alex looked over the side, seeing the giant pirate bobbing in the water, a dark writhing shape in the black sea that was soon left behind.

"Yes! Three for three, not *bad*, if I do say so myself." Alex grinned, going back into the pilot house, hurrying to find the key for the stateroom where the others were being held captive.

He powered the engines down to an idle, then looked at a large red button marked "anchor."

If I hit that button, everyone on the ship will know that we've stopped. But if I don't, the ship might hit something without someone at the helm.

Alex looked at the key in his hand, then the open door. "OK," he said. "This is what happens when you mess with one of the last 13 on their quest to save the world. Hope y'all are ready."

Alex hit the button and ran.

As he went below deck, he could hear the chains from the anchor already winding out. He hoped he could make it to the others before the anchors bit into the sea floor and brought the *Ra* to a jerking halt. That would alert the rest of the pirates that a mutiny was underway.

And I'm not sure I can deal with another nine of them on my own.

Alex sprinted as if his life depended on it. He slid down the stairs, his arms out on the rail and hitting the next level down in a second. He ran on. In the mess hall, six pirates lay scattered around the tables sleeping, having helped themselves to the spoils of the kitchen. Alex forced himself to stop and slowly tiptoe around them to the next set of stairs.

Hans' main cabin was there, and Alex took the stairs down quietly, the machine gun again in his hands like a baseball bat. Before he got to the bottom, the rolling hum of the anchor chains stopped.

Alex gripped the bannister as the three pirates guarding the door to Hans' stateroom saw him, springing to their feet, bringing their weapons up at the same time.

Uh-oh.

And then the *Ra* came to a full stop.

The sudden and unexpected halt knocked the pirates from their feet and gunshots rang out as they fell together in a heap, landing on their own weapons.

Alex let go of the handrail and used the butt of the gun to smash the glass door of a fire suppression system on the wall next to him. He pulled the handle.

Clouds of gas blasted from the roof, blanketing the room. Alex ran blindly, aiming straight ahead. He felt himself brush by the pirates as he crashed through their pile. He reached the door and used his hands to feel for the keyhole, unlocking the door. The door swung open, letting wispy clouds of gas into the stateroom.

Hans' rogue Guardians came storming through the blinding mist, rushing out into the hall to deal with the pirates.

"Alex!" Dr. Kader said.

Alex crawled towards the voice. The Egyptologist's face appeared, Hans close behind.

"Upstairs!" Alex shouted out to the German Guardians. "Six more of them are up there!"

Hans asked, "And the others?"

"Swimming in the Pacific."

"As to what this 'ultimate power' beyond the Dream Gate is, or even *where* it is," the news reporter was saying, "we are unsure. All we know, from information being confirmed by the spokesperson at the UN, is that right now the world's greatest hope of finding it rests on the shoulders of a fifteen-year-old boy named Sam."

Alex watched the news channel on the large television screen in the communications room on the *Ra*. The ship had been sailing south at full steam since leaving the last port, where they had delivered the remaining pirates to the waiting police. Alex had been so buzzed by the pirate ordeal and preoccupied with thinking about Sam's public revelations, that he'd forgotten to slip away to call his mother as he'd planned.

Since Sam's address to the UN, the revelations and speculations about Dreamers had been escalating, with attention turning to famous people and world leaders. A news channel had twenty-four hour commentary dedicated to Sam, speculating that he was everything from a clairvoyant to a superhero, a delusional troublemaker or a front for a secret crime organization.

"But it's the UN," Alex said to the screen as the "expert" commentators continued debating Sam's credentials. "Can't they see that he's telling the truth?"

"Sam's address to the United Nations again?" Dr. Kader said, heading over from his desk.

"Yeah, and all the commentary since," Alex replied.

The Professor had appeared at length on news telecasts, being quizzed about Dreamers and the secret battle raging around the world.

"Tell us again about this figure that calls himself Solaris . . ."

"Is it true that if you lose, we will lose our ability to dream?"

"Will we all be locked in a world of nonstop nightmares?"

"Who are the last 13?"

"Where did they come from?"

"Who's left—are they out there?"

"Are you one of them?"

And on it went . . .

Some programs started having competitions, seeing if they could uncover the remaining Dreamers of the last 13. All kinds of people were coming forward claiming to be the next Dreamer.

Alex muted the television and walked over to the port window. He watched the setting sun hitting the peaking caps of the angry ocean.

The water outside was a constant rolling swell and the *Ra* rose and fell as it sailed south as fast as the engines would take her. As a refitted icebreaker, the boat retained the capability to smash through thick sheet ice but had a ton of luxury thrown in for good measure. It was a five-star hotel on the water. All thanks to its owner, the billionaire Hans Schneider, leader of the traitorous German Guardians and, as far as Alex could tell, one of the "bad guys." Alex had agreed to come along on this voyage, under the guise of helping Hans, but really as a way to discover his plans and, hopefully, to stop the Dream Gate ever falling into his hands.

As they traveled further south, the weather grew colder. The Pacific Ocean was unforgiving as it sent eighteen-feet-high swells smashing against the *Ra's* strong hull.

"I'm going to my room," Alex said to Dr. Kader as he left the communications quarters. When he got there, he stretched out on his bed and got out his tablet. He'd manage to find a way to hack into the super yacht's comms system undetected, and could now report back to the Enterprise without having to sneak into the communications room and use the satellite phone. He smiled, thinking how all those countless hours messing around on computers had paid off.

Shiva would be proud.

He started up the program and waited a few seconds for the connection to establish. Then a familiar face flickered onto his screen.

EVA

The eleven Dreamers of the last 13 met in the Academy's basement storeroom, a dusty, dimly lit room barely big enough to seat them all amid the piles of student chairs, desks and outdated computer equipment. There were heavy wooden shutters over each of the narrow glass windows, all stuck tight with age and lack of use. The only light came from a bare bulb hanging from the ceiling by a tenuous, aged cord.

"I call to order the first secret meeting of the last 13," Xavier said in a mock-serious voice.

"Secret?" Rapha asked. "Why?"

Eva rolled her eyes at Xavier. "He's just messing around," she explained to the Brazilian Dreamer. "And as if we'd elect you as the leader anyway," she said to Xavier.

"Well, I *have* had a recent near-death experience," Xavier laughed, "so surely that gives me some kind of privilege, no?"

"But really," Cody said, looking around the room, "why are we meeting down here? Are we starting some lame 13 club now?"

"Pretty lame if *you're* a member," Xavier said.

Cody laughed, and it didn't take long for Xavier and then the others to join in.

"Nah, it's 'cause it's the only place we could think of where we'd be free to talk without being interrupted, or overheard," Xavier explained truthfully. "The common room is so packed, especially when Sam's there."

"Or Gabriella," Eva added, rolling her eyes. She looked around at all the faces in the room, lit by the glow of the lightbulb, as they continued to laugh and chat among themselves, taking comfort in each other's company. Only Sam remained quiet, just watching the group thoughtfully. Even though she knew each of the 13 had sought him out to pass on their condolences and support after what had happened in Cambodia, this was the first time that they had all been in one room together, and alone, since Sam's return. It felt good to be away from the curious and watchful eyes of the Academy's students and staff.

Eva suspected a barrage of questions was about to begin, and she guessed Sam could too, because he stood up to speak. The laughter and chatting died down almost immediately.

"OK, firstly," Sam said, "I'd like to apologize for my behavior these last few days. I'm sorry . . ."

"Sam, we underst—" Maria began to say, but Sam held up his hand to stop her.

"I know. Please, let me finish. Losing Tobias . . . he was . . .

well, it . . . it just hurts more than anything." Eva saw Sam take a deep breath and glance at Poh, who smiled calmly. "But I shouldn't have shut you all out. You guys are the ones who can probably understand the most. What—what I'm trying to say is that I know we still have a job to do. And I'm still willing to do it and I'm pretty sure you are too."

Everyone nodded in unanimous agreement. Sam turned to look at Eva and she met his gaze with happy tears in her eyes.

I'm so glad that he's come back to us.

"We're all here for you, man," Xavier said, his voice serious this time.

"To help you however we can," Arianna added.

"And to be there at the end when we need to," Zara said.

Eva couldn't stop smiling as Sam thanked all his friends.

"Group hug!" Gabriella said suddenly, the bubbly Italian grabbing on to Sam and squeezing him, and soon they were all crowded around him, locked in a hug of epic proportions.

"If only the United Nations were this united!" Cody said, tilting his head towards where the armored trucks would be circling the perimeter outside, keeping watch over them until the world's leaders could agree on what to do next.

The group laughed and dispersed, finding seats on cobwebbed, rickety chairs and on the floor.

"So, you know you're famous now, right?" Gabriella asked Sam. She was one of the few members of the last 13 who had been an international superstar *before* the race had started.

"Famous?" he said innocently.

"Yeah," she said, "not, like, just around here, but now everyone in the *world* knows who you are."

Sam shrugged.

"Maybe he hasn't seen it," Issey said, showing him a couple of web pages on his phone. "Since all this went public, the clip of you at the UN has had nearly one billion hits—that's huge. That's way more than I've ever had!"

"He knows," Eva said protectively.

"They don't care who I am," Sam said, "just what I represent."

Eva could hear the defensive edge to his voice, all humor now gone.

We have to look after him, help him get to the end of this race.

ALEX

"Hey, Mom," Alex whispered to the screen resting in his lap. His mother, Phoebe, could be seen smiling on the other end of the video call.

"Alex!" she said. "You said you would call me every day. What happened?"

"We, ah, had a little run in," he said tentatively, "with some pirates."

"What?!"

"Yeah. It was, ah, well . . . we're all OK now."

"Tell me everything that happened."

Alex gave his mother the short version of how they had been discovered by a rogue band of pirates at Nan Madol, before being hustled back onto the *Ra* and locked in a room while the pirates took control of the ship. He left out the part where he narrowly avoided a fight with the giant angry pirate.

"You should have left earlier!" Phoebe said, exasperated.

"Mom," Alex said, "I told you, it was no big deal. I didn't get this from the pirates," Alex said, pointing to the small graze still visible on his forehead. "That was from when the drones attacked the ship."

"A drone attack?!"

Oops.

"Oh, right . . ." Alex said. He calmly explained again, this time describing the voyage prior to when the pirates took over, when the *Ra* was fired on by Stella's missiles—the very reason for pulling into port for repairs in the first place.

"OK, I've heard enough. You're coming home and that's an order, Alex," Phoebe said fiercely.

"But I *have* found out more information," Alex said. "We're heading to Antarctica. I dreamed it—Hans did too. Did you know I have been having recurring dreams that I couldn't recall for years, about Antarctica?"

Phoebe was silent, staring at him.

"Mom?"

"No, we didn't," Phoebe confessed. "But that could also be because it might not be true. Hans will say anything to get—"

"Mom, I *want* to stay," Alex said.

Phoebe looked at her son, and could see how much it meant to Alex to be there, doing something he felt was important in the race. Without saying anything, she gave a slight nod of her head. "OK, so, tell me the itinerary," Phoebe said.

"We're docking at a city called Christchurch in New Zealand," Alex said, "taking on supplies, and loading some special equipment that is being flown in to meet us there. They've cleared the stern deck of everything but the load crane. You could fit a helicopter on there now. Then on to Antarctica, I guess."

"OK, call me again tomorrow. And, Alex?"

"Yeah?"

"Good work out there."

He smiled sheepishly. "Thanks, Mom."

Christchurch was a cold and beautiful city. Alex wandered the city streets, grateful to spend time on solid ground. He was shadowed by two burly German Guardians who were always close by, watching him, watching out for him. They'd even presented Alex with his very own German Guardian Stealth Suit in thanks for freeing them from the pirates. Glancing at his watch, he saw it was time to head back.

At the waterfront, the *Ra* was sitting lower in the water, and Alex could immediately see why—on the stern deck, in the space that had been cleared out, was a huge mass covered in tarps.

"Wow," Alex said as they walked along the pier to their berth. "Is that a helicopter or something?"

"Or something," the Guardian replied.

"A plane?" Alex said.

"No," the Guardian said.

"You're getting colder, Alex," the other Guardian said, and the two of them chuckled.

"Hmph," Alex replied, walking the gangplank to board the boat. The rest of the Guardians and crew were loading the last of the provisions. Hans was making sure the straps were secure on the mystery piece of cargo.

"What's that?" Alex asked him.

Hans stood, signaling for the crew to finish up and push off. "It's our ticket to another world," he replied with a cryptic smile.

"What," Alex said, "it's a space rocket?"

"Something like that," Hans said.

"Hmph . . ." Alex was *really* intrigued now.

What can it be?

"You'll find out soon enough—a little surprise every now and then is good for you," Hans said, laughing.

EVA

"The numbers don't lie," Gabriella said, waving her own phone, still obsessing over Sam's fans. "Look! It's just passed one billion, wow."

"They're interested in the *idea* of me," Sam said, "but this is hard for the world to understand. To them I'm either some kind of superhero or a delusional freak."

"Yeah, I guess," agreed Cody. "I guess it was hard for all of us to come to terms with the truth, about Dreamers and the prophecy and the race."

Eva couldn't help herself, the thoughts of Cody's surrogate parents and what happened in Denver springing into her mind. "Cody! I don't think you can really talk—"

"Cody's right though," Sam interrupted. "At first, most of us couldn't believe what was happening, and we were the ones having the nightmares. So how can the world get it?"

He's right, how can anyone possibly understand what this really means.

Eva could see everyone frowning in thought as she was, considering the significance of what Sam was saying.

The room stayed quiet for what seemed like a long time.

"Still, you *are* famous now," Xavier said brightly, breaking the silence. "That's pretty cool."

They all laughed again.

"Won't it be harder for you to do what you need to do," Zara asked, "with all the attention and everyone knowing what you look like?"

"Very hard," Arianna said.

"But it will be hard for Solaris too," Eva suggested. "And Stella and her Agents."

"Anyone else noticed that all the Guardians are gone?" Maria asked.

"Yeah, since yesterday," Rapha said. "I've not seen one."

"Maybe they don't trust them anymore," Xavier said. "And you can imagine why. They've had groups of them turning traitor and someone's been passing information about Sam to Stella this whole time."

"Sam, ever since your announcement in New York," Issey said, "the UN have been clueless about what to do."

"Maybe they are waiting to be driven by their own dreams?" Poh said.

"Look," Sam said. "I think . . ." he paused as if trying to sort out all the conflicting thoughts in his head before continuing. "I think it's always been up to us. That much hasn't changed this week. There's a reason why we are all sitting here in this cold basement, why we all feel so free to say whatever comes into our heads. Because, at the end of the day, you guys are who I can trust . . . and count on. The rest we can deal with when it happens."

"Yeah!"

"Let's do it!"

"We can do it."

"The only solution the world has come up with so far is to keep us here, 'protected' by the UN," Sam said. "They believe they're doing the right thing. But we all know that can't work. And the Professor knows that too. This race can't be stopped and we can't be in this race if we all sit around here."

"But what can we do?" Zara sighed. "We did not have time to find the missing Gears in the Doors."

"That's right," Xavier said. "And we never did get to try out some more superhuman abilities in the construct."

"Bummer," laughed Cody.

But Eva wasn't laughing. She was remembering the horror of watching Xavier having his chest pounded as the Doors doctors fought to bring him back to life. Thank goodness they'd managed it with barely a moment to spare.

We nearly lost him then.

"I know the Doors was a huge disappointment," Sam said, "but I'm sure we're all glad that *everyone* got out of Solaris' ambush in one piece, Gears or no Gears." He glanced at Xavier as the others gave him thumbs-up and smiled.

"Please, please," Xavier grinned, "enough about me, actually no, not enough, keep going!"

Everyone jeered good-naturedly as Xavier pretended to be offended.

"Anyway," Sam continued, "we've got to stay on track, and it's time for some of us to get moving again."

"Yes?" Rapha said.

"But the UN will never let any of us just walk out of here," Issey said.

Eva smiled. "Then we'll just have to *sneak* out," she said.

"Right," Sam said, grinning too. "Oh, and Eva has some other news."

"You've found the Dream Gate?" Maria called out.

The whole group burst out laughing.

"No, not quite that," Eva said. She looked at Sam, who gave her a small nod of encouragement. "But I have kinda found the next Gear, sort of."

The faces around the room were a mixture of relief, happiness and shock.

"I've had my dream," Eva said. "I'm number three."

SAM

No sooner had Sam returned to his dorm room after the group went their separate ways for the night, still excited about the news of Eva's dream, than there was a knock at his door. He opened it, expecting to find one of his friends there, but instead he saw Lora.

"Ah, hi, Lora . . ." Sam said, a little sheepish, thinking now that maybe he should have thought to ask her along to their impromptu gathering.

"Sam, we have news on Solaris," Lora said.

"Good news?"

"It's something you'll want to see."

"Now?"

"Yep."

"OK, sure," he said and followed her out.

They walked out of the dorm building and across the damp grass, and Sam very soon realized that they were heading towards the rowing shed, to Jedi's lab.

"They're still buzzing around," Sam said to Lora, gesturing up at the night sky and the flashing lights of helicopters. Media choppers from all over the world were competing for air space, all flying as close as they could to the UN-enforced no-fly zone over the campus in the hope of snapping photos of the last 13.

"Yep," Lora said. "And we're about to give them a new page one story tomorrow."

Sam wondered what she meant by that as they entered the boathouse and walked to a heavy steel door. Lora entered a numerical combination and then a thumbprint on a shiny security scanner and the door hissed open.

That's new. Jedi normally just leaves the door open . . . looks like we've got beefed-up security everywhere now.

"So, what's this news?" Sam asked Lora as they walked down the steep stone staircase.

"You'll see," she replied.

With each step, Sam's anxiety grew.

Don't be stupid. Solaris wouldn't be down here. They would have said something if they captured him . . . wouldn't they?

Sam settled his breathing and tried to relax.

"Are they ready?" he could hear the Professor's voice asking from around the darkened doorway.

Sam entered Jedi's computer lab and could see that the head of the Academy was not actually in the room—he was on a television monitor. On another screen was Jack, the Enterprise director, looking tense as he spoke quietly to someone off screen. Jedi was at the controls, wearing an earpiece. It was just him, and now Sam and Lora, in the room.

OK, so no Solaris. I knew I was being stupid . . . but, phew.

"They are on station," Jack said, looking directly at them now. "We are ready for go."

"I've just had confirmation from the field commanders, patching in audio now," Jedi said. "The teams are arriving at their locations."

On the wall in front of Sam a new screen had been installed. It was the biggest television screen he had ever seen, divided into several frames, all showing grainy video footage. The largest frame in the center of the screen showed an overhead shot of an island chain, the main island labeled Island X.

Surrounding that video link were ten smaller frames, each showing a very similar island scene of sand and green foliage, but all from slightly different perspectives. The images jerked shakily as though they were being captured by cameras held by people on the move.

Ten people, all moving fast . . . what is this?

"What's going on?" Sam asked.

"Ah, Sam," the Professor said, leaning forward on the screen as if to see further into Jedi's control room. "I didn't see you arrive. I am very glad you are here."

"Sam," Jack said from his screen, "we've tracked Solaris to this island location. What we are seeing right now is the real-time feed from a combined force of Agents and Guardians."

"All the people we could spare, from every corner of

the globe," the Professor added. "Almost two hundred personnel."

That's where all the Guardians have gone.

"Two hundred, converging on an island," Sam said, unsure he was hearing right, "to get Solaris?"

"That's right," Jack said, "We've split our troops into three teams and they are about to assault the hideout."

"Solaris has a hideout?" Sam said.

"He has to sleep somewhere," Jedi grunted.

"Through an extensive covert operation, we tracked him to this location," Jack replied. "We've been monitoring the island and saw him enter the location at 1600 hours, local time. He's still there."

"Wow, finally . . ." Sam said, his heart beating fast now. Lora stood by his side watching the screen intently, lips pressed together nervously. Sam looked from one video feed to the next, and it was clear now from the points of view that each camera was mounted on a helmet.

This is Guardian One. I am on station and ready for entry.

Guardian Two. We have eyes on the site, ready for operation in ninety seconds.

Enterprise Three. Designated target building in sight. On station in sixty seconds.

We read you, team leaders. Proceed with caution. Repeat, proceed.

Guardian One, copy that.

Guardian Two, mission's a go.

Enterprise Three, moving in now.

Sam watched as the screen flickered and switched to show more and more separate frames, now projecting the vision of over thirty helmet cameras. He saw that both Guardians and Agents were dressed in camouflage combat uniforms with helmets, goggles and bulletproof vests.

"What are they going to do when they catch Solaris?" Sam asked, looking at his two friends in the room. Neither Jedi nor Lora answered.

"I mean," Sam said, "it doesn't really look like they're there to *catch* Solaris."

"Sam," the Professor's voice said over the speakers, his face looking grave on the small screen, next to an equally serious Jack. "We must stop Solaris whatever way we can."

"But, you can't kill him . . ." Sam said, confused. He looked to all their faces for agreement. "I mean, we need him to tell us what he knows. What if he's hidden the Gears he has somewhere other than there? How will we find them? And killing him in cold blood will only make us as bad as him—won't it?"

"Sam," Jack said. "I understand your sentiments. We all have to make tough choices sometimes. There is no direct order to execute Solaris. But if we are faced with the choice between one life and that of potentially thousands, or even millions, which are at risk if he prevails, then I'm afraid we are really left with no choice at all."

Sam watched the operation unfold via the live footage being beamed from the field. Overhead imagery from small drone aircraft showed the three teams converging, two overland and one via the water, towards a small hut on the coastline.

"That's his hideout?" Sam said.

"That's the entrance," Jedi replied. He tapped a few commands on a touch screen and brought up a 3-D schematic of the island, zooming in on the hut, which was little more than a gateway to another world—a subterranean world. A maze of concrete tunnels snaked under the hut, leading to a massive chamber the size of a basketball arena.

```
Guardian One, breaching front door.
Guardian Two, entering air shaft.
Enterprise Three, scaling seawall, water entry
in sight.
```

Sam looked at the images from the helmet cams that now switched to green-colored night vision as the soldiers entered the underground world of Solaris' lair.

"Do we know for sure that Solaris is there?" Sam asked.

"A seaplane landed at the dock, which we had tracked from his last appearance."

"And you're sure it's him?"

"We had satellite imagery four days ago of him getting on the plane, and it's stayed put at the dock all week."

"But he might have gotten out somehow?" Sam said. "I mean, we don't know, right?"

"We won't know for sure until our teams sweep the complex."

```
Enterprise Three, we have secured the sea
tunnel, moving down to main level, no sign of
target.
```

```
Guardian Two, top levels secured, moving down
to main chamber.
```

```
Guardian One, all quiet here, we are at the
chamber air vents, ready to rappel into chamber.
```

"Copy that," Jack replied. "Proceed with caution."

Sam could hardly bear to look at the blurry vision of the dark tunnels. He felt like he'd spent a lifetime in tunnels recently, wondering what might be around the corner, what might go bump in the night.

Instead, he watched the 3-D model of the assault. The image of the compound was in crisp white lines on the screen, two hundred tiny red dots moving from three sides to converge on the main chamber.

The blast of explosions made Sam jump.

He turned to the screens that showed the Guardians' and Agents' footage. Most were obscured with dust and debris.

"Teams, report in!" Jack said.

The next minute was full of frantic radio calls as all the combined Guardian and Enterprise forces reported that they were OK.

`We tripped some kind of trigger. It was a warning system.`

"Then he knows we're coming . . ." Sam said, stepping closer to the screen, watching the helmet cams of the advance party as they crept onward to the main chamber. "I don't like this."

"Scans are reporting that there's no other movement," Jedi said, calibrating the 3-D schematic so that it zoomed into closer detail of the chamber. "No movement at all."

"That warning might mean Solaris is on the move," Jack replied. "Perhaps there is some kind of escape route."

"I don't think so," Lora replied, standing shoulder to shoulder with Sam. "He's either there or he's not. And if he's there, he'll have a plan."

"I'm worried," Sam said. "Either way, this is dangerous."

`Sending in some eyes.`

The Enterprise team leader took charge and a new image came up, being beamed back from a tiny camera aboard a small remote helicopter.

`And lighting up the room.`

She tossed what looked like a few tennis balls. Immediately, they began to burn with bright white light, illuminating the room.

The footage showed a room that was part evil-genius workshop, part storage warehouse.

"It looks like a hospital," Sam said, his nose almost up against the screen as he looked closely at the detail.

"There was an abandoned fort on the island before," Lora said. "It could have been a medical facility."

"No," the Professor said from his vantage point. "This is modern equipment."

"Maybe he's sick?" Sam said.

"Maybe," Jack replied. "But one thing looks certain. No one's home. Enterprise Three, move in."

`Copy that. Moving in. All teams, follow our lead.`

Sam watched the view from the helicopter hovering above the vast space as two hundred soldiers moved in, searching every corner and blind spot for a threat.

`Enterprise Three, the nest is empty. Repeat, the operation is over—no one's home.`

"Get as much as you can from the site," Lora said. "Make sure you take everything that looks like it might—"

"HAHAHA!" a maniacal laugh echoed throughout Solaris' chamber, the earsplitting sound amplified via huge speakers. "You pathetic fools . . ."

11

Sam swallowed hard and backed away from the big screen as though he might somehow get caught up in the action. The feed coming in from the helmet cams showed the Guardian and Enterprise teams were spooked, searching for a threat that they could neutralize.

"I hope all those watching this little show," Solaris' deep, metallic and raspy voice said, "enjoy what comes next."

Sam stood frozen, his eyes locked on to the screen, frantically hoping that Solaris was all talk, that the two hundred Guardians and Agents would get out alive and unharmed.

"ARGHHHH!" Solaris' scream, a battle cry, boomed out of the speakers and echoed around in the concrete chamber.

Half a world away, in Jedi's subterranean tech lab, the terror seemed just as real.

"No! Get them out!" Sam said, grabbing the microphone from Jedi's desk and shouting into it: "Everyone, get out! Get out of there!"

But it was far too late.

No!

Sam looked away from the screen as fire erupted everywhere, flashing across the helmet cams in horrifying clarity. It seemed to wash into the room from one of the walls, sweeping over everyone like a wave. Lora let out a gasp and grabbed Sam by the shoulders, holding him tight, trying to shield him from the view.

Jedi cut the main screen's audio and video from the site, transferring the visions to his computer monitor, but there was nothing left to see. After a couple of minutes of agonizing silence, he spoke quietly to the Professor and the director, the three of them desperately trying to contact anyone on the island but to no avail.

All communication was gone—there was no one left to respond.

"We've lost them," Jack said, his voice shaky.

"See?" Solaris' voice cut in, carving through the air like a knife. "This was just the *start*. You cannot stop me. I will be the victor. And then you will all bow down to the leader you deserve."

"That's where you're wrong!" Sam yelled out, his voice full of anger. He came up close to the microphone on Jedi's desk. "We will meet soon, and I will have the pleasure of smashing that mask from your face!"

The room was silent. Lora and Jedi were quiet, Jack and the Professor too, stunned by what had just happened.

Sam was shaking with anger, his fists clenched as though ready to fight.

"Yes, Sam," Solaris' voice scratched over the speakers. "We *will* meet, and soon. As to who will strike who—"

"Save it, coward!" Sam said, his neck and face flushed red with rage.

Solaris chuckled. "*I'm* a coward, am I?"

"You're the one hiding," Sam countered. "Where are you? Why don't you come out and fight like a man?"

"Like a man? I just took out all your hired guns," Solaris said. "I destroyed all those who might help you. You're on your own now, *boy.*"

"You're hiding behind your traps and technology and weapons," Sam said, "using them to do the dirty work for you! If you think pressing a button and killing all those people will stop us, you're even crazier than I imagined."

Solaris' voice sounded like he was smiling when he rasped, "And where are you, Sam?"

"I'm at the Academy, waiting for you, and I'm ready," Sam said, "any time."

"You won't do much good in this race stuck there, will you?" Solaris said. "Stuck in your cage with all the world watching their new pet."

"*Shut up!*"

"You have to get out of there, Sam," Solaris went on. "You have to get to Australia, with Eva, and I'd hurry up, or you might find that you're too late, again."

What?

How does he know . . . ?

"He's gone," Jedi said, tapping away at his computer. "He was transmitting his audio to the island from a remote location via a satellite uplink. No . . . I can't trace it."

"Then he could be anywhere in the world," Jack said.

"Yes," the Professor added, his voice heavy, "he could."

"No," Sam said. "He's on the move, headed to Australia. Or maybe already there."

"Sam," Lora said. "What are you—what was Solaris talking about? About Eva, and Australia?"

Sam felt the four of them looking at him.

"Eva has had her dream," Sam said. "She's next, she's number three. And her Gear is in Australia."

"I don't like it," Jedi said, after Sam had explained the dream and Eva was summoned to the lab to join the discussion. "I mean, how could Solaris have known about the dream?"

"The recording devices?" Jack said.

"I turned off the dream-recording devices here as soon as the UN surrounded us," Jedi said, "in case someone out there broke into the system and saw—well, saw things we'd rather keep secret. Somehow Solaris has managed to do just that. It's like he's got some way in that we don't know about."

"Maybe he does," Sam gasped. "I remember now—back in Denver, just before Solaris attacked, one of Mac's men said something about a suit being stolen, that Solaris was wearing it. Could that be it?"

"Do you remember anything else?" Jack asked, leaning forward intently.

"Only that they called it something specific," Sam said. "A flage suit, camouflage—no, *dreamflage*, that's it!"

"That certainly sounds like it might be how Solaris has kept up with us in the race," the Professor said.

"Some kind of tech that allows him to hack dreams?" Jedi said. "Could Mac have been working on something like that?"

"He would have had the resources," the Professor sighed. "It's possible that there's been something else in the mix all along that we didn't know about."

The silence in the room was deafening.

"And if Solaris is a Dreamer," Lora said, "if he's trained at steering dreams, at recalling them, at being there and taking it all in, then . . ."

"I really do have no hope of beating him," Sam said, looking at the blank screen, now devoid of life. "Maybe I shouldn't go out there anymore. Just have my dreams, tell you guys and stay out of it."

"It wouldn't matter," Jack said. "Solaris would still see your dreams and try to take the Gears from the next Dreamers."

"He's right," the Professor said. "In some ways, it's better that you *are* out there for the race for these final three Gears. At least you can take action on your dream right away when you're there and hope to stay at least one step ahead of Solaris."

"I guess a step ahead is better than a step behind," Sam said. "Still, I think this revelation just makes things seem even more impossible to win. It's like I don't know what to do anymore."

"Yes you do, Sam," Eva said, her voice defiant. "All of us, together, can beat him. And we're going to start, today, by going to Australia."

12

"**P**erfect," Lora said, taking a step back from her creation.

"Unrecognizable," Jedi said. "Lora, I do believe that you've missed your true calling."

Lora smiled at her handiwork. "What, you think I should have been a makeup artist?" she laughed.

"Or a disguise maker for Hollywood," Jedi replied.

"Well, I'm no Clark Kent," Sam said, looking at himself in the mirror. Lora had dyed his hair black and styled it differently, and he wore black-framed glasses.

"Well, that's just great!" Eva said. "I look like a geek! A complete dork."

Her transformation was more profound. Gone was her messily spiked black hair and heavy black eyeliner and dark lipstick, and in their place was her natural strawberry-blonde hair in a ponytail, her face clean save for some lip gloss.

"Wow, freckles," Sam teased.

"Arghh, leave me alone!" she said, pushing Sam away.

"You look . . . cool," Sam added.

"No, Sam, I don't," she replied. "And neither do you. You look like you're part of a lame boy band."

Sam appeared deflated.

"That's right," Eva said, "sucks not being who you want to be, doesn't it?"

"Right then," Jedi said, checking his watch. "It's three a.m., and if you're going to leave, now's the time."

"We're ready," Sam said.

"The sooner I'm out of here before anybody sees me," Eva added, "the better."

"Remember," Lora said, leading them to the ventilation tunnel that ran from Jedi's underground computer lab to a farmhouse ruin on the other side of the lake, "have your Stealth Suits switched to invisible until we're well clear. We still need to get across the open field beyond the farmhouse, which will be teeming with UN soldiers."

"Set them to optical and thermal invisibility," Jedi said. "They'll probably have heat scanners set up in anticipation of Stella's Agents. They've got next gen suits like these—without my tweaks, of course. And remember, these prototypes are not ready to be in the field, but we've run out of time to test them any more. Treat them carefully!"

"Right, got it," Sam said. "See you guys soon."

He led the way in a crouched run through the ventilation shaft.

"And if we get separated," Lora called out, "head for

Sweet Dreams Bed and Breakfast—it's in town, about five miles south of here."

"OK," Sam said as he kept shuffling along in a crouch.

"How are we getting to Australia, anyway?" Eva asked.

"With a little help from some friends," Lora replied.

Getting past the UN soldiers encamped outside the Academy proved no problem, given the hour. They'd walked through the rows of tents and vehicles, past sleeping soldiers, only a few of whom had drawn night watch and were huddled together, talking and laughing in hushed tones.

Great. We're the only thing standing in the way of the dream world being taken over and they're fooling around like this is some lame training exercise.

Just as they started to relax, there was a loud growl from behind them.

"Uh-oh," Sam whispered. They broke out into a run.

The dog barked as it chased them. It was a huge thing, a German shepherd, running full pelt towards them.

"Stealth Suits might make us invisible to the eye and infrared," Sam gasped, running next to his friends, "but we can still be smelled!"

"Speak for yourself!" Eva said, running slightly ahead of them.

"Make it over the fence and we'll be fine!" Lora said. They hit the chain-link fence, erected by the UN soldiers as an outer security perimeter, at the edge of the farmland. The three of them climbed fast, over the top, and dropped down on the other side.

The dog hit the fence hard, barking and snarling at them.

"Wow," Sam said, catching his breath. "That was close."

"Hey, who's there?" a voice boomed.

The three of them froze as a flashlight washed over them. It was a UN guard on a quad bike. The beam roved over them and found nothing, but it was unnerving to think that even up this close, they were completely invisible. They stood statue-still, not daring to make a sound.

The dog continued to bark, going crazy while the guard frowned and checked the fence again.

"Quietly," Lora whispered, "back away."

The three of them walked backward for five, then ten yards, up through the grassy bank that led to the winding road.

"OK," Lora said, still in a whisper. "Let's take the shoulder of the road into town."

Sam looked away from the dog, who was now quiet, chastised by his handler who probably thought it was tracking a rabbit or fox across the field.

They all kept their Stealth Suits switched to full invisibility, their appearance matching their surroundings until they got into the town.

They might not be fully tested, Sam thought, seeing the shimmer of his friends as they moved, *but they'll definitely do. Nice one, Jedi.*

"Across the road," Lora said, unveiling her head from the Stealth Suit's hood and then switching it to appear like she was wearing casual dark clothes. Eva and Sam did likewise.

"Follow me," Lora said, "and stick to the shadows."

13

EVA

The Sweet Dreams Bed and Breakfast was closed to customers, but a warm orange light glowed inside—a welcoming open fire. Eva cupped her hands to the window and could see two figures close to the crackling fire inside, talking animatedly.

Lora knocked on the old wooden door, and footsteps immediately hurried to open it.

"This place is owned by friends of ours," Lora said. "Past students of the Academy who settled here for a nice quiet life."

The door opened.

Dr. Dark stood there in the shadows.

We meet again.

"Lora," he said, looking up and down the street to make sure the coast was clear. "Something's just come up. Quick, come in."

By the fire was a huge man with well-tanned skin, clear bright eyes and long black hair. He strode over and shook Lora's hand, then looked at the two teenage Dreamers with what looked like awe.

"Sam, Eva," Dr. Dark said, "this is Jabari, the leader of the Egyptian Guardians."

"What?" Sam said, stepping back, taking Eva and Lora with him. "The *traitors*? What are you *doing*? Are you trying to get us all killed?"

Wait a minute, this is the guy from my dream. Why was I in a helicopter with him?

"Please, please," Jabari said, his voice deep and heavily accented. He came towards them with open hands. "You misunderstand, my friends." He bowed to them, catching them off guard with this sign of deference.

"It's OK, Sam," Lora said, pulling them back into the room. "Listen to him, please."

"I'm sorry, Sam, and Eva, for what some of my fellow Guardians have done in the past. For the sake of all of us, I hope that we can put it behind us."

"What? You want us to just forget you tried to blow us out of the *sky*?" Eva said accusingly. "I'm sorry, but that's a *lot* of trust you're asking for! Why should we believe you're now suddenly on our side?"

"You are right, of course. The Egyptian Guardians were the original protectors, the first Guardians sworn to protect the Dreamscape," Jabari replied. "We believed that stopping the prophecy was the only way to be sure the world would be safe. But now . . . most of us are gone, trying to stop the madman. These last few weeks as we have failed to prevent the prophecy, we have come to see we were mistaken. That this was not how to save the world."

"And now, what?" Sam asked.

"We reached out to Dr. Dark, and to your Professor," Jabari said. "We have admitted our wrongs and now we are here to set it right. There are only twenty of us left, but each is now sworn to protect you and what lies beyond the Dream Gate—to the death if it must be so."

Eva and Sam looked unsure, Eva eventually breaking the silence. "Let's hope it doesn't come to that. We're glad to have you on our side now."

Jabari smiled gratefully and shook her outstretched hand.

We need all the allies we can get.

Suddenly Lora looked around. "Where are the owners?" she asked.

"They'll be back soon," Dr. Dark said. "Don't worry, they're fine. We need to focus on getting Sam and Eva to their destination."

"What do *you* know of it?" Lora asked, suddenly alarmed.

"I'm afraid that Eva's dream is out there for many prying eyes to see," Dr. Dark said.

"That can't be," Eva said. "I mean, we've told no one!"

"The Professor and Jedi had all the Academy's dream recorders switched off specifically to stop anyone breaking in," Sam said.

"Stella can do it too," Jabari said. "She's managed to

get into the Dreamscape. She has a global dream-reading device online."

"And she can tap into anyone's dream?" Eva said.

Dr. Dark nodded.

"Via the old Tesla Coils?" Sam asked.

"In theory," Dr. Dark said. "We have tracked a signal to a site in the Ukraine that they are using to boost the Tesla machines to incredible power—*worldwide* power."

"The Ukraine?" Lora said.

Both Dr. Dark and Jabari nodded, and Lora looked into the fire again, lost in her thoughts. "What can we do about shutting it down?" she asked.

"We can tell the authorities," Dr. Dark said, "hope they go in with police troops, or the army, given it's a restricted zone, and arrest her."

"But by then it will be too late," Jabari said, his deep voice grave. "*Far* too late."

14

"Jabari's right," Dr. Dark said. "It will take them a few days by the time they put together a team, try to negotiate and storm the site—and then what? Battle her Agents for a few more days? They'll be well fortified there, they might be able to hold out for weeks. And that's beyond the time frame we're working with to get the Gears."

"*We* have to turn it off, it's our only option," Eva said. "We have to try. You want to take a team in there," she said to the leader of the Egyptian Guardians. "You want to make sure that Stella is stopped once and for all, don't you?"

Jabari nodded. "In a sense, yes," he said. "Although I do not think that *I* should lead the team there."

"Oh?" Lora said.

"No," Jabari replied. "I think *you* should lead my men."

Lora looked to Sam and Eva. "I need to protect them," she said. "I need to go with them to Australia."

"But together," Jabari said, "we can shut this down. The dream receiver, Stella, all of it. For good."

"There's got to be another way," Eva said.

"No," Dr. Dark replied. "I'm afraid not. There's more at play now. Powerful Dreamers who have been skeptical of the race now recognize Sam's importance. They're looking for him—the Zang family in China, the Mexicans, the Greeks. All the powerful dynastic Dreamer families, and they'll stop at nothing to get their hands on a piece of this action. Going public with this, Sam, may have been a mistake, I'm afraid."

Eva looked at their faces. *Great*, she thought. *Now we can't even decide what to do for the best.*

"OK," Lora said, then turned to face Sam and Eva. "Let's work with what we have now. The two of you go with the owners from here. They'll get you to where you need to go."

"But—"

"No buts, Eva," Lora said, then smiled. "These people? They're good people—the *best*. They're my parents. And right now we don't know who to trust. There could still be a spy in the Academy or Enterprise. But my parents? I *know* we can trust them."

"OK," Sam said. "We'll do it."

"OK," Eva said. She nodded but was far from happy with this new travel arrangement.

There was a loud noise outside. Eva looked out the window. It was Jedi's car, an old rust bucket he'd restored. He'd made one significant alteration, though. It was coated in the same material that made the new Stealth Suits invisible to the eye, capable of blending in with its surroundings. Two middle-aged people sat inside, waiting.

"That's my parents," Lora said. "They'll get you to the airport. And in that car, they'll get you past any roadblocks with ease. Stay safe."

She hugged the two of them and they all walked outside.

"So what's this place that Stella is using?" Sam asked Jabari.

"A devil's place," he replied, "a dangerous place."

"And why are you best qualified to lead the Guardians?" Eva asked Lora. "Apart from being super-tough, of course!" she added.

"Because I know the area," Lora said. "I've been there before, when I was a young girl."

"That's right," Dr. Dark said. "It's a place in the Ukraine, the only site in the world that can be used as Stella is using it. It's the site of a terrible nuclear disaster."

Lora looked at Eva and Sam and said, "It's Chernobyl."

15

SAM'S NIGHTMARE

I blink at a blinding sun and hold up a hand to shield my eyes. It barely helps. I'm standing at the top of a hill. There's dense foliage and water. It's a sea, I'm on an island. There are tropical trees, beaches dotted between cliffs. Several other specks of land are just in view. They seem smaller than this one.

"You guys are too late," a voice says.

I turn and see a friendly looking man dressed like a park ranger. A dark, ruddy face of someone who has not only lived his life in the elements but has ancestors who have for millennia. A name badge is sewn onto his shirt pocket—*Malcolm*.

"What do you mean?" Eva says. She's standing next to me, on the flat rock outcrop that forms a viewing platform over this idyllic paradise.

"What you're lookin' for," Malcolm said, "they moved that, years back, before my time even."

"How do you know what we're looking for?" Eva asks.

The guy breaks into a big toothy grin. "Because of that look on your faces," Malcolm replies. "I've seen it before, many times. My father saw it in his time, and his father, and so on, for hundreds of years."

"But we're too late?" I ask.

"Too late by a long shot," he says. "Still, all is not lost. Follow me—this island has a few secrets yet."

We follow the ranger down a barely visible path through the scrub. We're headed towards a rocky cove, the water breaking at headlands, the tide out, showing a vast stone shelf that has surely wrecked a lot of boats mistaking it for a calm harbor.

At what must be the tide line, we find a path that's more clearly defined.

"This looks ancient," Eva says, walking the narrow paved road.

"Yep," Malcolm replies.

Eva turns to me, she wants to know more, and I say to the ranger's back, "So, ah, what is it that we need to see that is not what we came for?"

"You'll see," Malcolm replies. He is a man of few words.

Eva looks back to me and I shrug.

We walk around the cove, following one of the headlands, and just before its point, we stop.

"Through there," Malcolm says.

He's pointing to where the smooth path carved into the stone disappears into a crack in the rock face barely big enough to squeeze through sideways.

"Are you serious?" Eva asks him.

"Not usually," he replies with a big smile. "But sometimes."

"Is this one of those times?" I ask.

"Yep, I reckon."

"Right," I say. "I'll lead."

"No, mate," the ranger says. "You follow her."

"What's through there?" Eva asks.

"It's a special place," Malcolm replies, looking absently into the yawning darkness of the cave. "Has been through all time. Though the rock must have shifted over the centuries."

"Why do you say that?" Eva says.

"Because," he says, "there's no way they got all that stuff in there through this little space. Maybe there was another way in once, and the land has hidden it. Mysterious, this island. But then, most places are, if you look at them right."

Eva takes a flashlight from her pack and squeezes through the rock fissure. I watch from the opening, and see the light getting duller and dimmer as she heads deeper.

"Are you guys coming or not?" Eva calls out, her voice distant and full of echoes.

I go to follow, but the ranger catches my arm.

"Let her have a moment in there first," he says to me.

I'm unsure what he means but I nod.

"After all, Sam," Malcolm says, his smile beaming. "This is her Dreamtime. We're just her guests."

"Run, Sam—run!"

No sooner have I made my way through the tightest squeeze of the cracked rock, than it opens up to a whole new world.

I look back and the rocks are gone. I'm now someplace else.

A whole new world . . .

An endless expanse of landscape is around me. It's hotter and drier than the island, and the scene is almost like the surface of Mars—barren, red rock gravel and rocks and boulders. The only things distinguishing it as part of the earth is the occasional scrub and brittle tree, a road and what looks like, well, like some kind of space station.

"Sam!"

Eva is pointing behind me.

I look, down the road. There are a couple of shapes coming at us.

Riders on quad bikes, kicking up dust plumes behind them. They're really hammering it—they want to reach us in a hurry.

I turn to Eva and we run across the red rocky ground, away from the surreal-looking space station compound, away from the bikes, away from the road. Eva's feet ahead of me are moving faster than I thought possible.

My head spins as I think maybe we *are* on Mars or some other planet, but I remember what the ranger, Malcolm, said before going through the rock—*I am in Eva's dream*.

"Eva!" I call. "Eva, stop!"

She stops running.

I do too. We stand together, panting for breath. The bikes are still speeding toward us, still on the road, maybe a minute away.

"Eva," I say, "this is your dream that we are in right now. You can control it, you're driving it all—the people chasing us, where we are, all of it."

"Right, of course. Why did I forget?" she says.

"Think. Why are we here? What did we come for?"

Eva's face creases in concentration for a moment. She smiles and looks down at her hands. They are palm up, one on top of the other. There's something bright and shiny there, glinting in the sunlight like a golden coin.

Only this is no coin. And it's far more valuable than any coin.

It is a tiny little brass Gear, actually two linked Gears, part of a machine. What we came for.

"I'm so sorry, Sam," Eva says.

I look up to Eva's eyes and see sadness and alarm there.

"I didn't know he'd be here until it was too late," she says. "I thought . . . I thought we'd lose him."

There is a presence behind me. I feel its shadow cast over me.

Solaris.

"It's OK," I say to her, fighting every urge to turn around or to run. "He won't harm us. He needs us."

"No," Eva says, and tears fall from her eyes. "He doesn't. Not anymore."

SAM

Sam woke.

He was still on the airplane. Eva was next to him, asleep. Her eyes were moving behind her eyelids—dreaming.

Part of him wanted to wake her, in case she was having a nightmare. But another part told him that they needed every bit of her dream that they could get if they were going to beat Solaris.

Sam pressed the call button and waited to order a snack and some water. He wiped his face with a paper napkin and opened up the air-conditioning vent above his head so that cool air washed over him.

Across the aisle, Lora's mother was reading a book. She looked up at Sam. "We've only been in the air an hour," she said. "You two must have been tired."

Sam nodded. The flight attendant arrived and he placed his order. Next to him, Eva still slept soundly.

And then Sam had an idea—about *changing the future.*

16

ALEX'S NIGHTMARE

I creep down the hallway, my feet silent. I open the door to Ahmed's workroom. There's no sign of the archaeologist, nor anyone else. I go inside and close the door behind me.

It's dark in here, but not completely pitch-black, the three round port windows at the waterline letting in some moonlight reflected from the sea.

I move forward in the dark, my feet shuffling carefully and my hands outstretched to guide my way. I feel the light box. It's a big solid structure, about the size of my Ping-Pong table back home. The sides are made of steel, and the top is opaque glass. I walk around it, my hands running along the sides, feeling for the power switch. I find it, flick it to "on." The lights are a bright-white, throwing eerie shadows around the room.

And it illuminates maps.

I look at the map on the top. It shows modern-day Antarctica—a map made from precise satellite imaging and plotting. The light box lets me see through it to the next map, and several more underneath it. Four maps altogether, from modern to historic to old and ancient.

I lean in close to see details, but they're hard to make out, so I lean in closer still—

I fall into the light box.

I fall *through* it, into another world. Everything around me is white.

Am I stuck inside the box? Am I in . . . ?

I shiver. My breath fogs in front of me. It's cold. I'm no longer wearing the tracksuit I had on. I'm now wearing a yellow snowsuit. The white around me is no light box.

It's snow.

Suddenly, I know.

I'm in Antarctica.

And I am alone. I turn around and see nothing but white. The ground is white, the horizon is white. I take another look at the ground as something has just registered.

There are other footprints next to mine. Turning around, I see the prints continue in a straight line, as though I walked to this spot with other people and stopped as they kept walking.

Why did I stop here?

Seeing nothing else around me, I follow the tracks, my eyes never leaving the prints in the snow. The wind blows icily and the weather seems to worsen. Soon ice and snow is being whipped at me and I raise my hands to shield my face. I'm crouched low so as not to be blown off my feet. I'm making slow progress, still following those prints.

A noise pierces the air.

What's that?

Howling, like that of an animal, is carried on the wind. I start to move faster. The sound is shifting, now it's coming from behind me. I turn around but I see nothing. It's getting louder.

Whatever it is, wherever it is, it's coming for me.
And it's getting closer.

I run down a hill, into fog. Soon I'm running blind.

I fall and slide, face first, down the slope. "Arghh!"

I close my eyes and wish I was someplace else and within seconds come to a stop when the ground levels off and the ice gives way to pebbles. I get to my feet slowly and painfully, and dust myself off. I'm under the layer of fog now and see that I'm at a lake. The water is unfrozen, steam rising from it as though it is warm.

"It *is* warm," I mutter as I take off my gloves and feel my face. It's warm to the touch. I walk to the water's edge and touch the pebbles—they're warm too—and then the water.

It feels like a pleasant bath.

"Ha!" I say. I look around. There's no sign of anyone else, of who I have been tracking.

Maybe they're smart enough not to get chased by some unseen beast.

The howling, screeching noise comes back as if in answer to my thought. Now it's from up high, up the slope, and it's moving, nearing again, fast.

Whatever it is, it's sliding down that ice slope like I just did.

I run along the pebbles at the lakeside. The sound behind me grows in intensity.

SPLASH!

Behind me something huge hits the water, and hits hard and fast.

I turn around to look.

And I'm knocked off my feet, the air sucked out of me, and I'm fighting to breathe as I look up to the white sky as the howling gets louder and louder.

"Alex!"

I get to my feet and dust off a snowball.

"Over here!" the voice calls. Sam is in the distance, pointing to something far off to my right.

I look around, disoriented at first and then in awe.

I am standing on a white cliff, and below is a vast sea full of icebergs. The horizon is moving towards me.

It's a wave. But no ordinary wave, this thing is huge, and it's rushing at us, pounding, seething.

A tsunami!

In seconds, it'll be here.

"Sam—run!" I yell. "Run!"

I turn to run but trip on the ground and land facedown on the cold hard ground.

ALEX

Alex woke up covered in sweat.

All he saw was a world of white. He pushed up, panicked, fighting against—

Bedsheets.

He pushed the white sheets away. He was in bed, in his stateroom on the *Ra*.

A dream . . . it was a crazy, mixed-up dream. What I saw didn't even make sense.

But was it a true dream? What if it was? What if my dream becomes real . . . ?

17

They got out of the taxi at the Sydney Opera House. Sam walked up the plaza a little and stopped, looking around. The harbor twinkled under the sunshine poking through the clouds, the water full of ferries, boats and water taxis coming and going—a big city busy as it went about a new day. Eva was at the water's edge, looking out across the harbor.

And no one recognizes us, despite being front page in the local newspapers.

Sam smiled.

Lora's disguises worked.

"What is it?" Eva asked, now coming over to stand next to him.

Sam turned to look at her, but noticed Lora's parents, Catherine and Ian, taking photos of the iconic Opera House. And then another figure, cutting a swathe through a throng of Chinese tourists. A big man, tall and dark.

Jabari.

"We're changing things around," Sam said.

"What?" Eva said.

"I had an idea, on the plane," Sam said to Eva, "and made a call."

"When?"

"On the flight, not long after we took off, when you were asleep."

"Why?" Eva said.

"So that he could tell me to come here," Jabari said in his deep voice.

Eva turned to face him.

"And, Sam," Jabari said with a smile, "I think this is a *good* idea."

"But—how'd you get here so fast?" Eva asked. "We only landed a couple of hours ago."

"Dr. Dark's jet," Jabari replied. "We'd just touched down in the Ukraine when the call came in. I took off again straightaway, leaving Lora there to head things up. And I came here."

"But, why?" Eva said. "To protect us?"

"To protect *you*," Sam said.

Eva's eyes searched his and he could see then that she knew. "We're splitting up," she said.

"We need to make different decisions to alter our future."

"If we change things like this—if we separate—we might not get there. We may not find the Gear," Eva said.

"This is a sound plan," Jabari said. "Lora, Dark, they all agree."

"Separating is a sound plan?" Eva said to them. "Change it another way."

"Think of it like this," Sam said. "Solaris can see into our dreams, right? I mean, right now, he's here already, somewhere in Australia, ready to pounce. That much we know for sure. So, how about we do this—I go to where you dreamed first. That'll change things up, long enough for us to get ahead."

"So that way Solaris will be confused," Eva said, the idea seeming to crystallize in her mind as a viable plan. "He'll be chasing an old dream and playing catch-up to the new version."

Sam nodded. "And Jabari will go with you," he said.

"I promise I will protect you with my life, Eva," Jabari said.

She motioned to Lora's parents.

"What about them?" Eva said, looking over at Catherine and Ian, who started to walk over, concern etched on their faces now.

"Why don't we leave them out of it? We've got a world to save," Sam said.

"Solaris doesn't yet know we are changing things," Jabari replied. "We have the upper hand now."

"Right," Sam said. "But he might see our changed intentions through any dreams we have now, find out who's with us and what we've changed."

"That's still a possibility, so we must make different decisions at every turn," Jabari said.

Lora's parents were reluctant to let Sam and Eva go, but could see the sense in their new plan. With promises to wait in Sydney in case they were needed, Lora's parents said their good-byes.

"Right," Jabari said turning to Eva, "where to?"

"Into the middle of Australia," she replied. "That's where the Gear is."

"You said we rent camels to get there, right?" Sam said, laughing.

"No," Eva replied.

"Come on, you two," Jabari said. "Let's go save the world."

The last Sam saw of Eva, she and Jabari were boarding a ferry and heading for Dr. Dark's jet at a private airport, where they'd be traveling as fast as it could fly to the town of Alice Springs in Central Australia.

Sam flagged a cab and headed back to the main airport. He was headed north, to a group of islands above the mainland that, according to the map on his phone, were tiny specks in the sea—the Wessel Islands.

His phone bleeped with a message. Sam looked at the screen, seeing a number he didn't know.

Sam, it's Alex.

I dreamed about you last night. We were together, near a coast, running from a tsunami.

Be careful. I think something bad is coming.

Sam replied.

Thanks for the heads-up.

Hope you're safe.

Where are you?

18

ALEX

Alex typed back.

Still on the Ra, headed south—to Antarctica!

Will update you when I can.

Good luck and be careful out there.

He hit "send."

He was curled up with a quilt around him. The sea was rough—the roughest he'd ever encountered, and the seasickness pill he'd had that morning didn't seem to be working. The port window in his cabin was crusted over with ice on the outside and condensation inside. It was a gray sky out there, angry foaming waves smashing against the *Ra*'s rocking hull as they sped south.

His phone bleeped again.

You be careful too!

Be wary of who you trust. And stay in touch.

Alex replied.

Will do.

And right back at ya.

He hid his phone under his pillow and went to the galley

to find some different anti-nausea medicine that he'd seen there before.

"Ah, caught me red-handed," Hans said, fixing himself a towering sandwich. "Hungry?"

"No—no way, thanks though," Alex said, making a face at the food and turning a shade of green. "I'm seasick. I just came looking for something to settle my stomach."

"Ah, here, take this," Hans said, shuffling across the moving deck, rummaging through a medical cabinet and tossing Alex a bottle of motion-sickness pills. "Extra strength. I used to be like that too, when I was about your age. A few years in the navy soon fixed that."

"You were in the navy?" Alex said.

"The German navy, just like my forebears," Hans said, slicing the massive sandwich and then picking up a piece. "I thought it the right thing to do, at the time. Turned out that was not the life that was destined for me."

"Because you were a Dreamer?"

"Yes, in a sense," Hans said through a mouthful. "Though I was a lousy one, I discovered. I went to the Academy, the same Swiss campus that you were at, but it did not work out for me. I was too disbelieving, too rebellious. So instead I became what I figured was the next best thing to being a trained Dreamer."

"A Guardian?" Alex asked.

"Ha!" Hans snorted and Alex turned his eyes away from his gaping mouth. "Good lord, no. I went into business for myself! An entrepreneur, using my Dreamer advantage to the hilt, of course."

"So that's how you got so rich?" Alex said.

"My family, as Dreamers, never really, shall we say, *played by the rules,*" Hans said. "The Academy teaches students to use their dreaming skills for the benefit of *all.* You know, like creating new vaccines, improving how we get power—like splitting the atom."

"That was not exactly a benefit, was it? I mean, not *purely* a benefit."

"Not in the sense of it then leading to the creation of nuclear weapons, no," Hans said. "But you get my point, yes?"

"Einstein's work can be seen as a benefit if you consider nuclear energy as a relatively clean source of energy," Alex said, "but it's a double-edged sword."

"Yes." Hans moved on to the second half of his sandwich. "For me, such Dreamers showed what we could do, if we were driven. It became clear to me, Alex, what I *could* do— and what I *should* do."

"Make your family even richer? Become a ruthless treasure hunter?"

Hans chuckled. "My family owns many patents on inventions and ideas and discoveries made over the centuries. I simply continued that process. Sure, we made a *lot* of money along the way, I'm not ashamed of that."

"Then what's in this race for you?" Alex asked. "You don't

need any money that will come with finding the Dream Gate—or power. With all the money you have, you can buy any power you want."

"No, I do not need money. Nor the power that money can buy."

"But you're doing this, on your own. You betrayed your friend, Dr. Dark, right? Why are you not working with the others?"

"The others? Like those at the Academy? Like those at the Enterprise? Dark? Solaris?"

"Well, yeah."

"We all want our own destinies to play out, Alex," Hans said. "I believe that it is my destiny to be the one to open the Dream Gate. I've worked my whole life to have a chance in this race. Even if that cost me a few friends, like Dark, along the way." Hans paused. "I want to be there at the end. I want to see with my own eyes what this so called 'ultimate power' is."

"We all do," Alex said. "We all want to be there. To see it firsthand, to experience it."

Is Hans really all that bad? Is he any different from the rest of us who want to be at the Dream Gate?

But the question is, if he gets there first, what will he do with all that power?

Hans smiled. "Exactly, Alex. Exactly."

"What I want to know," Alex said, "is why we're going to Antarctica? What's there that's so vital? Do you really think the Dream Gate is there? What—buried in the ice?"

"It may be, Alex, it may well be," Hans said, wiping his mouth. "But we won't have to wait much longer to find out."

19

EVA'S NIGHTMARE

The sign before us simply says—THE VAULT.

"This is it," Sam says. He goes to a control panel and starts to punch in numbers.

"How do you know the code?" I ask.

"I don't."

"Seriously?"

"Seriously. I don't. *You* do," Sam says, entering more numbers. "You gotta trust yourself more."

"You're right," I smile. "The code relates to a word. The key is knowing which numbers are attached to which letters."

"*Now* you're getting it."

Sam steps aside to let me key in the sequence.

There is a noise behind us—footfalls on the concrete floor. Someone's crashing the party and they're in a hurry.

"Eva, they're coming!"

BRRRRR.

The digital dial makes a noise and a red flashing light comes on.

"No, wrong numbers!" I say. "Quick—what are the numbers for 'thirteen' if X is one—"

PANG!

A dart hits the wall next to my head.

I turn around to see two of Stella's rogue Agents rushing down the corridor, their dart guns pointed right at us.

THUD!

A dart, fired at my back, hits my raised forearm. The Stealth Suit protects me, the dart hitting the fabric and bouncing off harmlessly, the ceramic barb broken.

BING!

"We're in!" I say.

The dial is lit up with a green light and the vault door hisses open. We run through and together shove it closed behind us.

PING! PING!

Darts bounce off the outside of the door.

CLONK!

It's closed. I turn to Sam.

"Beat them again," he says with a smile.

We turn around.

My heart skips a beat. I raise my arms to protect myself and close my eyes . . .

I open my eyes and see I'm tied to a chair in a dark room.

Stella is standing across the room. The space around me is dark and cold, and there's a dull light globe hanging from the ceiling. It's swinging slightly on its cord. The swinging light casts weird and scary shadows in the room. There are no windows that I can see, just a single door. There might be other people in here, lurking in the deep shadows.

All I can see is Stella in front of me.

And another person, seated. A guy with dark hair, his head slumped down so I can't see his face.

But he seems familiar.

He too is tied to a chair.

"Tell us where the Gear is, Eva," Stella says, holding the guy's hair in her fist so that she forces him to raise his head.

Sam!

He has a puffy and bloodied lip like he's been in a fight. He looks tired, worn out and can hardly focus. His black-framed glasses, part of his disguise, are still on, but one of the lenses is broken.

"Don't tell her anything," Sam manages to say.

"Ah, still has a little fight in him," Stella says. "Look, you two are going nowhere until we get what we came for. We know you've been in the vault, so where did you hide it?"

I don't reply.

Sam is silent too. His eyes kind of go side to side, as if to say *whatever happens, don't tell Stella a thing*.

"Look, Eva," Stella says, her voice eerily mean and calm at the same time. "You know we're not leaving here until we have the Gear, so make this easy on yourself—on Sam. Look at him. He can't handle much more. Save him, save *yourself.* It's just a piece of metal. Tell me where the Gear is."

The Gear? We had the Gear?

A tall man steps from the dark shadows of the wall. I can't see his face in the swinging light, but he seems familiar and scary.

His hand rises to Sam. I recognize the black shimmering suit, the flame-shooting apparatus wrapped around his wrist.

"Turn up the heat," Stella says.

Solaris laughs through his mask. He takes aim. A flame lights up the darkness.

"No!" I scream. "No! Leave him alone!"

EVA

"Eva . . . Eva!"

Eva opened her eyes and felt Jabari shaking her shoulder. His face was friendly, his eyes clear and alert.

"Where are we?" Eva asked, sitting up straighter and stretching out.

"We're on Dr. Dark's jet," Jabari replied, "and we've just landed in Alice Springs."

"Already?" Eva looked around.

"You slept the whole way," Jabari said.

"Wow."

"Did you dream?"

"Yes—yes I did." Eva's dream started to trickle back into focus. The fog of sleep was still snaking through her mind. Then her expression changed as she realized. "And what we're doing now will stop that from happening. We're changing the future!"

"Good. With any luck, Sam is doing the same, and at the very least we buy enough time to get the Gear and get out of here."

Eva nodded.

"Do you know where we need to go?" Jabari asked.

Eva looked outside—the heat was visible, shimmering over the tarmac outside, and beyond, the ground of the airport was orange-red earth, a foreign landscape in a foreign land. She turned to look at the Guardian. "Yes, I know where."

ALEX

"It's called the *Osiris*," Hans announced with grandeur. "It's a deep-ocean research submersible. It can take six people, plus equipment, underwater for up to twelve hours."

"It's awesome!" Alex said, running a hand along the sleek orange hull. There were four thrusters at each end, looking a little like desk fans, but evidently powerful enough to propel the submarine through the water. Floodlights were lined along the sides, interspersed with video cameras and six long mechanical arms—two at the bow, one on each side and two at the stern.

It looks like a giant bug.

Each arm had a claw, as well as other attachments.

A blowtorch? A grappling hook launcher? This is the coolest thing I've ever seen!

"It won't do the Mariana Trench," Hans said, making way for the crew to attach cables to the crane, "but the *Osiris* will handle the depths of the ocean floor around Antarctica."

"The Mariana Trench," Alex said, recalling the maps he'd seen in Ahmed's stateroom, "is nearly three and a half miles deep."

"We don't need to go down that far," Hans said with a smile. "In fact, we don't have to go down far at all. But we do need to travel *under* the ice sheet. Her hull has a specially reinforced outer casing which will protect us if we bump into the ice."

"Why are we anchored here?" Alex looked across at the snowcapped rocky islands, the shores and outcrops pounded by the angry Southern Ocean and littered with fat seals, soaking up the sunlight.

"Sea trials for the *Osiris*," Hans said, giving the go-ahead for the crew to lift the submersible and move it over the water. "I'd much rather we do a final systems check in calm and shallow water here than where we're going."

"This is *calm*?" Alex said, looking at the waves smashing against the rocky outcrops. He peered over the edge of the ship. The water was so deep it was black. "This is *shallow*?"

"Compared to where we are going," Hans said, "yes."

The *Osiris* touched the water gently, a crew member climbing aboard and detaching all the cables except the tie ropes. Two men went aboard via a ramp.

"They're the pilots," Hans said. "Best in the world."

"Cool," Alex said, watching the submarine bobbing around like a cork.

Least it'll be calm under the water, right?

"Ready?"

"Ready for what?" Alex looked at Hans.

"Surely," Hans said with a smile, "you want to go for a ride?"

Alex looked back down at the submarine, which now looked tiny next to the super yacht. "Yeah!" he said, clapping his hands together excitedly.

"Then follow me," Hans climbed the ladder down to the hatch. "I've been waiting to see your sense of adventure."

Ahmed was the last aboard the *Osiris*. The hatch shut and there was a scraping noise as it sealed and the cabin pressurized.

"We're ready," Hans announced. "Commence with sea trials."

He, Alex and Ahmed sat in seats that faced the side walls of the sub, which were covered in controls and display screens that showed images from the hull-mounted cameras all around the *Osiris*.

"Yes, sir," the pilot said. "Taking her down fifteen feet and moving south of the *Ra*."

"Very well," Hans said. "Make it so."

Alex swallowed hard and watched the blank screens before him.

When the cameras come online and I can see what's out there, it'll be OK.

"I always wanted to say that," Hans said, making a sideways grin at Alex. *"Make it so!"*

"Yeah, that's great," Alex said, his palms sweaty as he held tightly on to the harness over his shoulders.

You always wanted to go on a submarine, so get a grip, Alex.

There was a gurgling noise from outside, and looking over the pilot's shoulder out the front window, Alex could see that they were going under. This close to the surface, the daylight penetrated enough to see a school of mackerel flash by, their silver sides shimmering like glitter.

It'll be cool. Just relax and enjoy the ride.

"Flood torpedo tubes one and six!" Alex called out, then laughed. "Ready the countermeasures!"

The pilots of the sub laughed. Ahmed gave Alex a look as though he was sure Alex was going nuts.

"I'm joking!" Alex said. "Come on, Ahmed—have a little fun! Have you never wanted to be on a submarine?"

"No, not really." Ahmed looked ill. The archaeologist was sweating too and looked spooked. His normally tanned cheeks were ghostly pale.

"Ahmed?" Alex said as the whine of the thrusters picked up in volume. "You OK?

Ahmed nodded but remained tight-lipped.

"It's just a test dive," Alex said, as much to reassure

himself as Ahmed. "Just a test dive . . . it's going to be awesome. I'm sure Hans has spared no expense."

"No expense!" Hans said.

Ahmed nodded.

"And we're not going down deep," Alex said.

"Deep enough," Ahmed replied. "I'm afraid I'm not very good underwater. It's unnatural."

"Ah, my good doctor," Hans said over his shoulder. "What's unnatural is a man of your profession wishing to stand on the sidelines while the great discoveries of the world are made by someone else. Sometimes one needs to step out of one's comfort zone to achieve greatness, do you not agree?"

Ahmed nodded and Alex could see that he was trying to settle his breathing.

The thrusters went quiet.

"Preparing to dive," the pilot called out. "Taking her down to one hundred fifty feet."

The copilot relayed messages through his radio headset to the *Ra* above.

Alex sat with his legs tense, pushing against the hull wall and pressing himself tight into his seat. He could hear the whoosh as water was let into the ballast tanks and the *Osiris* started to descend. Ahmed's hands were tensed on the control panel in front of him.

"Passing sixty-five feet," the pilot announced. "Eighty. One hundred . . ."

"The bottom here is at two hundred sixty feet," the co-pilot said. "Going through one fifty, slowing descent."

"Leveling out at one sixty-five," the pilot said, adjusting controls. "We have neutral buoyancy, level at one hundred sixty-five feet."

Alex heard the thrusters engage, muffled now that they were underwater.

"Switching on cameras," Hans said, fiddling with controls.

The screens in front of Alex and Ahmed came alive, changing from solid black to the inky black of a dark underwater world.

"Main floodlights coming online," Hans said, flicking switches. "Hull lighting is operational and so are the cameras."

Suddenly the screens were showing a world of blue and green.

"We're in a cloud of krill," Hans said. "Karl, take us along the ridgeline."

"Yes, sir."

Alex watched as the world outside slipped by with serene beauty. The krill, illuminated by the floodlights, swirled like ink in the water. They broke through and a rocky ridge was below them, long wavy sea grass on the shallower side towards the islands, the dark abyss of the ocean on the other.

"It's incredible . . ." Alex said.

"Try your camera controls," Hans said.

Alex took the joystick and flicked between the cameras, seeing the view from each side and every corner of the submarine. He zoomed in on a dark shape moving through the sea grass.

A sea lion burst through, its face coming right up to the camera, smiling, inquisitive. Alex tracked the camera around in a circle and the playful creature did a full three-sixty roll, almost cross-eyed as he watched the lens.

Alex laughed, Ahmed too.

"Sir, we'll have a visual on our objective soon," the pilot announced.

Alex frowned.

Objective? Wasn't this a test dive, to test that the sub's systems were working?

"Good, take us right over it," Hans said. "Do a sweep from bow to stern to find the captain's quarters."

"Objective?" Alex said. "What is our objective? The captain's quarters of what—a ship?"

"Well, Alex," Hans replied, his eyes never leaving the screens in front of him. "You see, this is a test dive, true, but it is also so much more. It is that *and* a recovery mission."

Huh? What could we possibly recover down here?

SAM

Other passengers were already standing in the aisle, their carry-on bags over their shoulders and in hand, waiting impatiently for the doors to open.

I never get why they are in such a hurry, pushing and shoving.

"Welcome to Darwin," the flight attendant said as Sam exited the aircraft.

The heat and humidity hit him. He didn't bother walking across the tarmac to the terminal, where the masses headed to get their bags and line up for taxis. Instead, he flung his small backpack over his shoulders and made a beeline for a sign that read "Northern Territory Helicopter Charters." Waiting in line, he was skipped over a couple of times as the receptionist helped out groups of tourists booking pleasure flights.

"Can I help you?" she asked Sam, looking at him as though he were lost.

"I need to get to the Wessel Islands," Sam said.

"This is a *private* helicopter charter service," the woman said. "We cater to people willing to spend a lot of money for a once-in-a-lifetime travel experience."

"Yes, I'm sure it is," Sam said, and he took his wallet from the backpack and handed over the Academy credit card in all its shiny golden glory. "You see, I'd like to book a private helicopter for the next day or so."

"Day or so?" she asked, her eyes locked on the card.

"Yes," Sam said. "Twenty-four to forty-eight hours should do it."

"Oh, I see, sir," the woman said on running the card through her computer scanner. "Just one moment, let me check our system and see who might be available. And it was to the Wessel Islands, right?"

The helicopter flashed over the crystal blue sea.

"Just up here," the pilot said, pointing ahead, "the Wessel Islands."

"Is there a spot to set me down for a couple of hours?" Sam asked.

"Mate, you've booked me for the next couple of days," the pilot said, keeping the helicopter low, skimming sixty-five feet above the waves. "I'll set you down, pick you up, fly you around, whatever you want. I'll fly you to Disneyland if that's where you want to go."

Sam laughed. "That won't be necessary," he said. "Just a few hours on the island."

"Which one?"

"The biggest," Sam said, looking at the map on his phone and reading from the screen, "Marchinbar Island."

"No worries," the pilot said. "I'll set you down on the southern beach. Good fishing there—not that you brought rods."

"Next time," Sam said over his radio headset.

"You sure you'll be OK out there on your own?" the pilot said. "Ain't nothing out here but beaches and a bit of wilderness, and a small station on the northeast side."

"I'll be fine, thanks," Sam said.

"If you say so." The pilot brought the helicopter over the widest part of the beach, circled around and set them down.

"I'll be back in two hours," the pilot said. "I'll go wait on the next island, Rimbija. I've been wanting to try some fishing over that side."

Sam gave him a thumbs-up and kept his head low as he made his way clear of the rapidly spinning rotor blades.

Once the aircraft took off and was clear, Sam took off his shoes and changed his Stealth Suit to a T-shirt and board shorts. He walked to the water's edge, the sea lapping over his feet and ankles.

Waiting time.

"Hey," a voice said.

That was quick.

Sam turned around.

A familiar guy dressed in a ranger's uniform of khaki shorts and shirt was standing next to him. He was an indigenous Australian, his dark face creased with age, partly hidden behind a big bushy beard which revealed a wide smile. They were meeting for the first time but it felt as though they'd been friends for a long time.

"Nice day, eh?" the guy said.

"Yep."

"I'm Malcolm." He thrust his arm out and they shook hands.

"I'm Sam."

"Sounds about right," Malcolm said. "I've been waiting for you to show up here. But I was expecting two of you. She's not coming?"

"You mean Eva?" Sam asked. "No—we, uh, decided to change our plans."

"That'd be a good idea," Malcolm said.

"So, you said you were waiting for us?"

"Yep, about long enough, mate. Come on, I'll show you what you came for."

"It was right here," Malcolm said as they moved through another section of the beach, "they found some copper coins. Back in 1944, Arabic inscriptions on them, would you believe? Found just lying here in the sand."

Sam drank from his water bottle thirstily, listening to Malcolm's story as they walked.

"It was the Second World War then, but after them Japanese bombers attacked Darwin, these little islands were in a good position to help protect the mainland," Malcolm said. "One of the soldiers stationed here found them. Turns out they were from an island off East Africa and more than a thousand years old."

"Coins that old in this part of the world?" Sam asked, surprised.

"Yep. Their discovery was shocking, to say the least, since most people believed that the first European who came to Australia was some Dutch sailor in the 1600s."

"So the coins prove that someone came here before that?"

"More than someone," Malcolm said. "*Lots* of people—

travelers, passing through on their ships, sailing an ancient trade route that stretched over dangerous seas from Africa to Asia and Australia. And over a long, long time they came and they traded and rested here."

"Not that I mind hearing about Australia's history," Sam said, "but what is it that you have to show me?"

"What do you think it is?"

"Something to do with my dream," Sam said, looking around at the edge of the beach where rocky cliffs towered over the sea. "A hidden cave?"

"Yep. We're here because of a dream you had," Malcolm said, "and a dream Eva had."

"You know about it?" Sam said. "You know we were in a dream—you were really there?"

"Yep."

"So you're a Dreamer too."

"We're all dreamers, Sam," Malcolm said, smiling. "And what I have to show you is a bit more exciting than a handful of old coins."

Sam looked around at the rocky landscape that jutted out into the endless sea.

"We sometimes have people come through, archaeologists and whatnot, snooping around," Malcolm said. "It wasn't coins they were after. But I didn't show them this."

"What is it?" Sam asked, scrambling over the rocks, hearing the sea crashing on the rocks below.

"A sacred place for my people," Malcolm said, climbing, "but over time it became a bit of a place to keep things too. We call it the Source."

"I've seen it before." Sam looked at the fissure in the rock wall. It was in a sheltered rocky cove, right on the waterline.

"But you didn't see where it went," Malcolm said, "did you?"

"No. We went through and we ended up someplace else."

"That's what it does," Malcolm said. "You go in there and it will show you where you need to go."

"Really?"

"Yep. If you're willing to see, then you find what you're looking for."

Sam looked at the dark cave. The tide was turning, and the water would soon cut it off and flood the cove.

"You're not coming?"

"Nah, mate, I've seen it. I'll wait right here," Malcolm said, sitting on a rock and looking out to sea.

Sam set off, leaving his backpack behind. The first squeeze in was easy enough, though a few feet in, the cave turned and became tighter. He breathed out, making his chest smaller, and pushed through. If not for the flashlight, it would be completely dark, and the floor of the cave went down, wet underfoot from the flooding it received each day.

He was reminded of the cavern he'd found with Maria back in Cuba, where they'd discovered an old pirate ship.

"Wow."

The flashlight showed the ground rising ahead of him, this time with steps. A waterline showed that where Sam was now standing would be completely submerged at high tide. It would appear like an impassable flooded section of the cave.

A water lock to keep people out.

Climbing the stairs, he emerged into a chamber.

Actually, this isn't like the one we found in Cuba.

Not even close.

This cavern was much, much bigger.

And he was not alone.

EVA

Eva and Jabari moved fast across the dusty ground. Aside from the light spilling out of tourist cabins nearby, the only other visible feature was Uluru, or Ayers Rock, the largest sandstone rock formation in Central Australia. At any other time, Eva would have stopped and taken it all in—snapped photos, looked at the plants and animals, sat down to enjoy the wondrous sight before her.

But not today.

I'll come back another time for the sightseeing tour.

Assuming there is another time to come back. Right . . .

They snuck into the plush resort, their Stealth Suits matching their environment, making them almost invisible to the naked eye. The soles of their shoes left imprints in the dry red dirt outside as they ran past the swimming pool to an access hatch hidden among the scrub.

"You're sure this is it?" Jabari said.

"Yes," Eva replied. All around them was the resort, little cabins ringed around a pool. Behind the admin building, the hatch had metal louvers and was set over a concrete base no larger than an office desk. A humming noise was coming from inside. "It has to be. This bit I remember from my dream. This is part of the underground facility that we have to get into and getting in this way means we're changing things from my dream. I mean, why break in when you can *sneak* in?"

I'm turning into the queen of sneaking around.

"OK, hang on, I'll do this." Jabari took a power screwdriver and undid the casing on one side. Next he put his head in and had a look inside. There was a clonk, and then the humming noise stopped. Jabari pulled his head back out. "There was a large extractor fan which I've disabled, and under it, through the grill, I can see a corridor."

"See?" Eva said, smiling. "Ye of little faith."

"Follow me," Jabari said, and he tied a rope to a nearby fence post and tossed it down the open air vent and shimmied down. "I'm in, come on down."

Eva followed, squeezing through the vent, then dropped to her feet on the concrete floor below. In each direction, the corridor seemed to go on forever, the overhead lights on sensors, only flickering on where they stood.

"Which way?" Jabari asked.

"Towards the Rock," Eva said.

They set off at a jog, the lights above them coming on as they ran past.

Eva looked back and saw the lights turning off again.

That's good. If someone else comes along, we can hide and the lights will go off and not give away our position.

"Hey," she asked, "think these sensor lights will pick us up if we switch our Stealth Suits to invisible?"

"Worth a try," Jabari said, and the two of them changed the Suits in one fluid motion, never breaking stride.

The lights continued to switch on.

"The sensors are either very sensitive," he said, "or, for all we know, they could be picking up our weight on the ground."

"Great," Eva said, then checked over her shoulder again, feeling what she imagined was a breeze, as though a door at one end of the vast corridor had suddenly opened.

What she saw made her trip over.

Jabari stopped and helped her up to her feet and she pointed down the corridor.

In the distance, the lights were switching on. Someone was coming. And judging by the ever-increasing speed at which the corridor was being illuminated, they were traveling fast.

Really fast.

SAM

The other occupants of the cave were bats. Thousands and thousands of them, hanging from the ceiling.

Sam remembered the massive bat colony he'd seen in the Grand Canyon. Here too there was a cool sea breeze passing through, coming over his shoulder from where he'd entered and escaping someplace ahead.

"So there's another way out," Sam murmured to himself.

He climbed to the highest vantage point in the cavern and stopped.

The place was filled with barrels and ceramic and metal urns, the beam of his flashlight picking out the glittering gold of doubloons and the shimmering steel weaponry of an ancient era.

"And a—sarcophagus?" Sam made his way down to where he saw what looked like a gilded coffin. Up close it was indeed that, covered in crystals that shone as he wiped off the dust and grime.

"What on earth *is* this place?"

A sound started up, like a whistling of the wind, and he followed it. The stone stairs led down to another antechamber, and he found himself in another space, similar to one he'd seen before in Japan. Sam's flashlight picked out the crystals in the rock of the granite chamber, a bench-like pedestal presiding in the center.

Sam realized then what Malcolm had meant about seeing what he needed to.

This cave isn't just a place for precious treasure. It's like the room in Japan—this is a conduit to the Dreamscape.

Sam sat on the carved granite seat, the surface smooth and solid. He settled into as comfortable a position as he could, closed his eyes and relaxed, willing himself to sleep.

The room lit up.

SAM'S NIGHTMARE

I am in that land of red dirt again. I am looking directly at the space station, some way off in the distance.

Not Mars—Australia.

I startle as I see Henk, the helicopter pilot, next to me. The rotor blades kick up the dust as the helicopter sits on the hard ground.

"Do you know what this place is?" I ask.

"I know it's a government facility," Henk says, "and this is as close as I can take you. They warned me over the radio to stay out of the immediate airspace or they'd shoot me down."

Shoot us down? What kind of top-secret stuff is going on here that they'd take such serious action?

"Yeah, thanks for getting me this close," I say, looking back to the massive compound.

"I think my friend Eva is in there."

"Then you'd better go help her," Henk says. "You get out, give me a holler. I'll be right here, waiting."

"Thanks."

I walk down to a dirt road and start the long trek in.

Near the gatehouse, where a security beam blocks the road, a dog starts barking. A big dog, by the sound of it.

Great, more dogs.

A uniformed guard comes out and eyes me suspiciously.

"Hey," I call out. "I'm lost."

"Sorry, kid," he replies as I near. "We got nothing for you here. Nearest town is somewhere out that way." He waves in a vague direction behind me.

I nod.

"Say," the guard says, walking closer, then looking over my shoulder and down the road, "how'd you get out here—you walk?"

I see the dog is chained up. It's another German shepherd. I smile at him, and he almost seems to smile back, like he's obeying my wish to be nice.

I'm in a dream, I can control what's happening.

"Yeah, I walked," I say to the guy. "And I'm going to walk in now, and you're going to show me to my friend."

The guard looks at me, puzzled for a moment, then says, "Ah, yeah, no worries, I'll show you around."

"I'm going to want to see where you keep the really secret stuff."

"Yeah, of course, follow me," he says. "I'll show you to the vault."

"The vault," I say, walking around the barrier and giving the now placid dog a scratch behind the ear. It looks like it's ready to roll over and beg. "Does it have a code or key or something to unlock it?"

"A code."

"Can you tell me the code?"

"I'm not cleared to know it. Right this way."

I follow the guard to a low building, practically no bigger than my old bedroom, but made of concrete. There are no windows, just a single heavy steel door. The guard swipes his ID pass through a scanner and we enter.

Inside is another wall with another set of doors and a call button, which the guard presses.

The elevator opens.

He presses 3B.

We descend and the doors open onto a world of shiny metal and bright lights, of endless expanses of computer equipment and screens.

"This is the operation's nerve center," the guard says. "The vault is just down here."

We walk along a steel mesh gangway over the servers and computers and through another door. Beyond is a platform that looks like a small subway station and I see that it is in fact a monorail link, similar to one I've seen in Seattle. But this one is underground.

"Where does this go?" I ask as we climb aboard a bullet-shaped car that looks like it came right out of a theme park, complete with the padded metal bar that locks down over our shoulders. I rap on the window, marveling at the thick, reinforced glass.

We're not going into outer space, surely . . .

"This takes us to the vault site," the guard replies. He

points over his shoulder. "Go the other way, you get all the way to the North West Cape submarine station on the coast."

"But—isn't that a huge distance away from here?"

"About thirteen hundred miles," he says. He presses the "canopy close" button, then pushes the throttle forward.

I feel like I have left my body at the platform, shocked, as we travel faster than I have traveled on land.

Maybe in the air too.

I gasp at the sheer velocity we are moving at, my brain struggling to catch up to my body as it hurtles underground.

The headlights of the maglev monorail light the way on the round concrete tunnel and we flash along at simply phenomenal speed. It seems like seconds but it takes maybe five minutes when a chime sounds and the guard eases off the accelerator.

I feel myself getting dizzy, and the world around me shifts a little and grows brighter.

I'm starting to wake up.

I squeeze my eyes shut.

No, I'm not ready, stay in the dream longer . . .

"We're here," the guard says.

We step out onto a platform the size of a basketball court, and beyond that is a lit-up gangway that we walk across, a vast lake beneath us, the water sparkling in the light. But there is also a deafening sound—more water, rushing fast. We're in the biggest cave that I've ever seen.

The roof is out of sight above us, the far side is nothing more than a pinprick of light at the other end of the suspended bridge. Below us is a lake and leading somewhere from it, a raging river.

"Where are we?"

"Under the Rock," he says.

"The Rock?"

"Uluru."

"What *is* this place?"

"A communications station—they found the cavern, and the water, by accident when they began drilling to put in the antenna."

"Why would you put an antenna *underground?*"

"To communicate across large distances. We run power from the moving water down here—it's like an underground hydro plant."

"And why's this vault located here?"

"Because that's where we found it. When they were drilling test cores and they discovered the chamber—"

The world around me starts to crack and shafts of light pierce the cavern's darkness.

I'm waking up!

"The vault?" I ask quickly.

"He's the guy," the guard says, pointing. "Looks like he's opening the vault for someone now."

We jog across the final stretch of the platform, skidding to a stop as the people standing there turn to us.

But this man is not alone. There are two people next to him.

One is Eva.

The other is Stella, holding a gun to Eva's head.

ALEX

Alex pressed his nose up to the screens and was surprised at what he saw. It was huge, unmistakable, incredible. The powerful floodlights of the *Osiris* lit up their objective like a movie star on the red carpet.

It was another submarine.

Alex watched the footage as more and more of the wreck was revealed by the cameras. They were looking at an old submarine, and it was big—easily ten times as long as the *Osiris*. It must have been wrecked long ago, now covered in barnacles and full of sea life. As the *Osiris* swept along the wreck's length, it became clear that it was settled on a ridge, where the edge of the island chain disappeared underwater and tapered off into a seemingly bottomless abyss of dark ocean.

"What is this wreck?" Ahmed asked. "Why are we here?"

Alex was surprised that the Egyptologist had been left out of the information loop too.

"This is a German U-boat from the Second World War," Hans said, his voice full of reverence as he saw the ghostly wreck emerging from the gloom of the deep cold sea. "My grandfather served on this vessel on its final mission."

Alex watched the screen in front of him.

Is this a sightseeing trip to honor his grandfather's watery grave? Can't be—Hans said this was a "recovery mission." What could be on this old wreck that is so important that Hans would interrupt our journey to Antarctica?

"This is no test dive," Dr. Kader said. "Far from it."

"That's right," Hans replied. "This is a retrieval mission." He spoke to the pilots, who took the craft slowly to a point just forward of the tower. Alex's monitor showed the side mechanical arm was outstretched, running the length of the vessel, and a beeping sounded in the cabin.

"That's it," Hans said to the pilots, the Geiger counter lighting up and making a contact crackle over the *Osiris'* speaker system.

"You are looking for radioactivity?" Dr. Kader asked, pointing at the gauge.

Hans nodded. "Take us forward three feet, Karl, then keep us steady while I cut into the hull."

"Yes, sir."

"Don't worry," Hans said, feathering the controls of the outstretched arm. "We are simply looking for a radioactive marker."

"Marker for what?" Alex asked. He jumped back from the screen as a huge eel flashed by the camera's lens. "*On what?*"

"Near the end of the war," Hans said as he selected new equipment at the end of the claw, "this U-boat was converted into a transport craft. They used it and others like it to take a large shipment of priceless artifacts and relics to Antarctica. And, importantly for us, they mapped where they took it, including the dangers they encountered along the way. That map is stored in the captain's safe."

Hans stopped talking while the *Osiris* drifted down the hull of the U-boat.

"Adjusting for currents," Karl called out. "This area has unpredictable water flows. We should try to be as quick as possible down here."

Alex saw Ahmed swallow hard, sweat starting to drip from the tip of his nose.

"Keep us steady," Hans said. "Give me ten minutes, in close and as steady as you can."

"Yes, sir. We're getting a current coming up the abyss wall and hitting the warmer water. Doing our best. You can try using the extra claws at the seaward side to keep us steady, they at least have a propeller."

"What—you're talking to me?" Alex said, seeing the pilot nodding at him. "All right!"

Alex took the twin joystick controls and got a quick rundown from the copilot as to how to operate them.

"Just keep her steady as you can." Hans returned to his controls once the craft settled. "No one knows," he said, picking up his story, "where the final resting place of that

Antarctic drop-off was, as it was recorded only on a map within the captain's log which was left on the ship. It carries a radioactive marker so that in an event such as this, it might be found. All hands were lost on the submarine."

"You're trying to get a captain's log that's been underwater for decades?" Alex said, squeezing the triggers on the thrusters to fight the current.

"Yes."

"Why?" Alex said. "Do you think your grandfather shipped something to Antarctica that we need?"

"Perhaps," Hans said, working the blowtorch's bright-blue flame in the water. Bubbles erupted from the red scar of molten steel hull as he cut into the side of the old submarine. "But the last communication, before they set off, was that the place had ancient ruins. And to find it, we need that log."

Ancient ruins—in Antarctica?

Alex stole a glance at Dr. Kader, who was still stressed at the prospect of being so deep underwater.

"My grandfather was a smart man . . ." Hans paused as he wrestled with the controls, the sub fighting to remain still against the current. "If we can retrieve his log book, it will make our trip to the end of the world that much easier."

Hans started up the blowtorch once more. Alex watched the screens in front of him, hypnotized by the bright torch blazing away at the thick steel.

26

EVA

"They're gaining on us," Jabari said and stopped running.

"What are you doing?" Eva gasped. She could see their pursuers now—there were angry-looking guards in a small jeep, another one coming up behind them. The front guards were yelling, one of them waving what looked like a gun.

"I'll hold them off," Jabari said, "you go get the Gear!"

"No, I can't!" Eva said.

Jabari looked at her with a stare that would make a grown man tremble.

"I don't want to leave you behind . . ."

"Eva," Jabari said, "this is my destiny—it's been written in the stars long before you and I were ever dreamed of." He gave her a gentle push. "You must go now, otherwise all will be lost."

Eva gripped Jabari's arm tightly, forcing herself to nod.

Then she turned and ran.

The lights of the corridor flickered on, but she was ahead of them, constantly running into darkness, leaving the light behind.

She risked a quick glance back and was relieved to see one of the cars had somehow stalled, the occupants still, on the ground.

Jabari.

Eva smiled. She didn't know if Jabari was still in the game, but he'd whittled the odds down to even money, the second car still in pursuit.

One against one, I'll take that!

Then Eva paused and nearly tripped.

The second car got close enough for Eva to recognize the driver.

No . . . it's Stella!

Eva ran on, willing herself towards the door that she could see just up ahead.

Eva jumped from the bullet train car, silently thanking her dream. She used it to outrun Stella and she smirked when she thought how angry that would have made her.

Now I've just got to get to the vault.

She slunk quietly in the shadows, but there was no one around.

Guess they figure they don't need guards around here.

Eva hurried across the steel bridge. She moved in a low crouch, wary of someone seeing her progress. The sound of her feet moving fast across the steel mesh was drowned out by the water gushing into the underground river.

And here I am.

Eva stared at the vault door, forcing herself to slow her breathing and concentrate.

Just like in the dream, just like I knew it then. The answer is "thirteen."

She slowly spun the dial, counting to herself. "If X is one, then T is twenty-three, H is eleven, I is twelve . . ." her fingers found their way, clicking through each number.

"And last is . . . seventeen . . ." Eva held her breath as she waited for the door to open.

Nothing.

She looked at the large handle next to the dial.

Right, of course.

She pulled it down, setting off the mechanism, gears crunching within as the door heaved open gently on its massive hinges.

She stepped into the vault.

The ancient red rock walls were in stark contrast to the sleek modern shelves that filled the vault. Numbered steel drawers rose up before her as she spun around the room seeking inspiration.

"OK, last 13 dream," Eva sighed to herself, "where do I look?"

She closed her eyes and concentrated, letting her mind drift back to her memory of standing right there. A minute passed, feeling like an eternity, but when she opened her eyes, she was smiling.

Passing all the shelves and drawers, she went to the back of the vault, searching for what she knew she needed. A ladder.

Perched on the top step and trying not to look down, Eva let her fingers gently sweep across the roof of the vault, ochre dust gathering on her fingertips.

"I know you're here," she murmured, "don't hide from me."

And then she found it. The smallest of lines, a crack in the rock face. Next to it, a carving in the stone—III.

Number three. And here I am, centuries later, ready to take what has waited for me all this time.

As she pressed on the carving, a narrow slit opened above her head and she pushed her open hands underneath it, deftly catching the small cloth package that dropped straight out.

Yes!

27

ALEX

A cascade of bubbles erupted on the screens in front of Alex and the *Osiris* rocked in the water.

"Hold it steady!"

"We *are* steady!" Karl said, some panic in his voice. "It's the U-boat—it's shifting!"

"What?" Hans said and stopped work to change the images on the screens. The cameras now showed the long U-boat rocking and twitching where it had laid still for so long.

"Cutting out that panel has disturbed whatever balance it had on the ridge," Hans said.

"We're going to lose her!" Karl said. "It's listing towards the abyss, you have two minutes, max!"

"Then we have to act quickly," Hans said, his voice calm. "Alex, come over here!"

Alex unbuckled his harness and moved up to the seat next to Hans.

"Take the controls for the forward arm and follow my lead," Hans said.

Alex did as instructed. It took him a few seconds to

work out the movements of the arm, and soon he had it next to Hans', the pair of them moving inside the old sub.

On the mechanical wrist joint of each arm, a piercing light and camera system showed the inside of the vessel.

"It's moving again," Karl announced. "You have a minute twenty."

The *Osiris* shook as the arms were knocked sideways from the movement of the shifting U-boat.

"Hans," Alex said. "What are we doing?"

"This," Hans said. The vision in front of them erupted in a shower of bright-blue bubbles again as the blowtorch cut through an internal door. "Use your claw to attach and pull the door away."

"OK," Alex said. The bubbles disappeared and he maneuvered the arm to the door, clasped the handle and started to retract the arm. "It's not working! It's stuck tight."

"One minute!" Karl called out.

"Give us full thrust away from the U-boat!" Hans called out. "Alex, hold the grip tight."

The *Osiris'* thrusters worked as one, biting into the water with all their power and driving them away from the old submarine.

A long, squeaky, tearing noise traveled through the water and echoed into their hull, like a giant beast howling in the water as the metal of the door tore away.

"That's it!" Hans said. "Take us closer and keep her steady!"

"I'm trying but we're fighting the up-current!" Karl said, wrestling with the controls as the *Osiris* jerked in the water.

Hans guided his clawed arm through the open doorway and into the captain's quarters, the footage from the mounted camera showing a clouded view as the movement of the old wreck disturbed many decades of silt. "Alex—keep the pressure on that door."

"I got it," Alex said, watching Hans' monitor, the German guided by the quickening bleeps of the Geiger counter to find his way.

"Thirty seconds!" Karl said. "We pull away in thirty. The sub is going to go over the edge!"

"Got it!" Hans said. The video feed showed the face of a steel safe, the size of a household microwave, against a wall. The claw latched on to it, and Hans shifted it back.

The vault didn't budge.

"Alex, I need your help with this!"

Alex manipulated his mechanical arm so that it kept the door propped open with one of its two elbow joints, while the claw shot forward and gripped next to Hans."

"That's it, Alex!" Hans said. "On my mark, drag the safe back with me. Three, two, one—*now!*"

Alex pulled back on the claw controls and the safe pulled free, the bolts tearing from the floor as though it were made of cardboard.

"Twenty seconds and we're outta here!"

"Almost there. This is heavy, help me out with it, Alex!"

Hans said. They used both claws to remove the safe. "Got it. Give us full thrust away!"

The thrusters whined in unison, their power at full throttle and the *Osiris* shuddered against the strain.

CREEEEEAKKKKK!

The old U-boat tilted on its side as the small sub moved away from it. Both crafts shifted as one, tilting further towards the abyss, the U-boat nearly on its side and the *Osiris* under it, as though hanging on upside down. Alex and Hans had their feet pressed against their side of the hull.

"More thrust!"

"We're trying!" the copilot said.

WHOOSH!

As more air left the buoyancy tanks, the *Osiris* sank.

SNAP!

"Get us away from the wreck!" Hans yelled.

"We're outta here!" Karl said. He engaged full thrust to get away from the craft, so much so that they were now falling faster than it was. "We're getting free. Now dropping weights for rapid ascent."

"Alex," Hans said, "keep the claw arm clear as we—"

The U-boat shifted further on its side and slid down the ridge—right on top of them.

Hans' claw remained on the steel handle of the safe and carried its weight, quickly bringing their cargo towards the *Osiris*, while Alex's mechanical arm was caught inside the wreck.

"It's stuck!" Alex said.

"Detach the arm," Karl commanded.

"Ditch it!" Hans said.

"How?"

Hans hit the emergency release button—but it was too late.

The *Osiris* rolled in the water, the claw still inside the U-boat, tearing it off. The sub rocked and rolled.

Alex, unharnessed, was thrown around like he was inside a washing machine. He hit the control panel screen in front of him. As he slid into unconsciousness, the last thing he heard was the *Osiris'* emergency alarms blaring.

28

EVA

Eva closed the vault door behind her and spun the dial, turning it from green back to red. The Gear, the smallest she'd yet seen and made up of two pieces, was now hanging on her dream catcher necklace, woven in tightly to the charm, almost a part of it.

Looking for another way out, she opened the door at the far side of the vault. A small corridor led to some kind of recreation room, with bathrooms, couches, a table tennis table, television and vending machines. The only other door from there led back to a ramp that headed down to the steel bridge.

OK, so one way in, one way out.

Looking back the way she came on the bridge across the water, the place seemed deserted.

Eva was exhausted. Her feet felt like heavy weights. She could no longer sprint and could barely jog.

Come on, Jabari, where are you?

Eva started walking, her feel clanging quietly on the steel.

She stopped.

There were other footsteps. Someone was coming up from the bridge but she couldn't see anyone.

"Jabari?" she whispered.

No, he wouldn't approach her invisible like this.

It must be Stella!

Eva turned and ran back, thinking maybe she could climb one of the steel ladders she'd seen that led up to a vast ledge holding huge concrete water tanks.

Behind her, the clanging of running feet continued.

Panicked, Eva looked around.

Stella was still nowhere to be seen.

"Don't hide from me like a coward!" Eva shouted defiantly.

"I'm not," Stella said up close.

Before Eva could react—she was knocked to the floor.

Stella stood in front of Eva, her arms crossed, her face pulled sharp. She was swinging Eva's dream catcher necklace idly from one hand. Eva forced herself not to look at it.

She's already gotten what she wants and she doesn't even know it.

"We can *make* you talk," Stella said, a tight smile on her face. She opened a briefcase and removed a headset, holding it out for Eva to see. "This passes a current to the prefrontal cortex, which then overrides your brain. We increase the plasticity of your brain, make your synapses fire faster and open a gateway for us to see into. Want to try it out?"

Eva remained silent.

"We can get deep into your mind with this, in ways you will not enjoy."

Eva looked away.

"Last chance," Stella said, taking the few steps towards Eva and crouching down so that she was level with Eva's face. "Tell me about your dream, tell me about the Gear, or things get messy. If I have to go in that head of yours and dig, you'll start getting all kinds of weird memories."

"Get messy?" Eva said, defiant. "What, you're going to spook me with your boring, predictable attitude and bang on about how you want to rule the world? *Please.* Go bully someone else."

"Eva, Eva, Eva," Stella tutted, standing up and flicking a button to change the image on the screen. "Do you recognize this place?"

Eva looked at it. It seemed to be footage from a video camera. The view was of an abandoned military installation of some sort. Stella touched another button to show a new view from on high, looking down at a crumbling ruin of a city.

"No? How about these images?" Stella scrolled through different camera angles.

Eva recognized none of it. The state of decay of the place was odd. It looked maybe twenty or thirty or forty years old, no older, the forests that surrounded it slowly taking it over. Roads were split with tall trees growing through the cracks. Most of the windows in the buildings were broken. It was deserted—a ghost town.

"How about this one?" Stella said.

The next image showed a group of people moving through the streets. They were walking a tight formation and they had weapons. There were maybe twenty people. The camera zoomed in on the group.

First there was Lora's face, then Xavier's and the Egyptian Guardians.

"It's Chernobyl," Eva whispered.

Xavier? What's he doing there?

"Very good," Stella said. "Now, would you like to talk, to tell me everything about your dreams, to save your friends?"

Eva watched as the group were slowly nearing the first building Stella had shown her—a dull gray metal military structure. That's where Lora and the others were headed.

"You tell me what I want to know," Stella said, "and they can leave in one piece. You don't talk? Well, you can see what will happen to your friends, yes?"

The image changed to a new vantage point—this one showing a large group of people, at least fifty or more.

Some in vehicles, and all with weapons. These were Stella's remaining Agents. Ready and waiting for her friends.

Lora, Xavier . . . they're walking straight into a trap.

XAVIER

Xavier checked his radioactivity badge for what felt like the millionth time. It still showed yellow, which was not as good as the green it had showed a few hours ago when they'd entered the site. But at least it wasn't orange or red.

When it gets to red, I'm outta here, no matter what's going on. I don't care what my dad reckons. Safer with Lora? Maybe, but not this time.

"Up here!" A squad of the Egyptian Guardians called out to them.

The Egyptian Guardians are mean machines, we'll be OK.

Xavier and Lora jogged up the block to join them.

"There's no movement we can detect," the squad leader said.

"OK," Lora replied. "Take your team to the control room and rig it up, and have the second squad move through and place charges all along the structure, starting at the first joint up there."

She pointed up high. The thing was enormous. A metal wall of steel beams and girders and wires, bigger than any of the long-abandoned apartment towers around here.

Maybe it's the biggest antenna in the world . . . it's just that no one's been anywhere near it for decades. Until recently.

"And have the third team move in with the vehicles and wait for us all back at the entry point," Lora said, "so we can meet the others on the road and get out of here by the time it blows."

"Got it," the team leader said, and he spoke rapidly into his tactical mic.

"Set all charges for thirteen minutes," Lora added with a smile.

"Thirteen minutes, copy that," he said, leading off with his three colleagues, running towards the antenna control tower.

"Thirteen minutes?" Xavier said. "That's a nice touch."

"I thought so."

"Stella's really tapping into the Dreamscape with that?" Xavier asked.

"Yep," Lora said. "Least, she's trying to, and will be able to soon."

"What happened here?" Xavier asked. "Like really, not what they tell you in history class."

"They amped up the power so much, trying to make the system read dreams on a global scale, it blew the reactor core."

Xavier shuddered. "This place really creeps me out."

"It's called Chernobyl-2, but we used to call it the Steel

Yard," Lora said, looking up at the structure. "Back when I was a kid, I heard my parents talking about it. It was part of the Russian version of the Enterprise, long gone these days," Lora said.

Xavier looked up at the scaffolding, seeing the ground team lacing the metal uprights with sticks of dynamite. He checked his radioactivity reader again.

Nearly at orange.

"Relax, we'll be out of here soon," Lora said.

They walked to the center of the road and looked up at the crew moving their way along with the explosive charges.

"And you've been here before?" Xavier asked.

"Yep," Lora said. "My parents brought me here once."

"That's some family vacation," Xavier chuckled, looking around.

Lora laughed. "It wasn't like that. They wanted me to see with my own eyes what had happened here. It's a strong example of how sometimes Dreamers' ideas can get the better of them."

"What is it?" Xavier said, aware that Lora looked suddenly on alert.

"It's quiet," Lora said.

"It's a nuclear wasteland," Xavier said. "What are you expecting, a parade?"

"Something doesn't feel right. Come on, let's take a closer look around."

SAM

It had been several hours of flying south and two refuels since Sam had said good-bye to Malcolm, and he thought back to their final conversation, when they'd said good-bye at the beach.

He remembered Malcolm telling him about the sacred site, and how he was a part of the last people to keep hold of what used to be the "old way."

"Old way?" Sam said.

"We all used to be Dreamers, a long, long time ago."

"How long?"

"Longer than you or I have been around," he smiled. *"Longer than our people as we know them have been around."*

"Really?"

"Our ancestors, those who came before my people. A mighty race."

"Where'd they go?"

"Ice age hit. The world changed. Races migrated and all that."

"Who built this?" Sam asked.

"Not my people. It's far older than that."

"Older? Your people have been here for thousands of years."

"This is an ancient land—older than any of us. These carvings show that a battle between good and evil played out far earlier."

Henk, the pilot, broke Sam out of his daydream. "So you think your friend Eva is walking into a trap, eh?" he said.

"Yep," Sam said.

"Well, you're just gonna have to save her, then," Henk said.

"That's right."

"But all on your own?"

"I don't have any other options right now," Sam said.

"What can I do to help?"

"Help?"

"I saw you on the news," Henk said. "I reckon I believe all that stuff you said, at the UN. Helping you out is the least I can do. Maybe it's *my* destiny, right?"

Sam looked surprised.

"I've always been good with faces," Henk winked.

Sam smiled. "You could create a diversion for me."

Henk smiled back. "You got it. Whatever you need, mate."

"In that case . . ."

The compound was a speck on the horizon. The sun was low and the huge white domes reflected the last remaining light. Henk explained they were called radomes—protective coverings for the equipment underneath, which were probably huge radar dishes.

"Do you really think there could be underground water out here?" Sam asked, skeptical of his dream. As far as the eye could see there was nothing but dry earth and sparse patches of green scrub and trees that had adapted over millennia to the arid environment.

"I reckon there's water under there all right," Henk said. "A whole boatload of it. If water comes down from up north and out east and forms an underground water table, it could be big, *real* big."

A warning light on the helicopter's dash lit up and started to beep. "OK, mate, it's a no-fly zone from here," Henk said. "I'll circle around the edge of it."

"You know, I've got a better idea."

"I can't go in there. They'll shoot us out of the sky before we have time to argue with them," Henk said, banking the chopper to the right. "I've heard stories about this place. Looks like you'll need to go under it. Walk in, or hitch a ride, but it's a long way, and it's going to be a hot night."

"You don't need to enter the restricted airspace. Just take us up as high as possible and let me know when you need to turn back," Sam said, climbing between the chairs and into the rear cargo hold.

"What are you going to do?" Henk asked. "Jump out?"

"That's *exactly* what I'm going to do," Sam said.

The wind buffeted inside the cabin.

Sam looked to Henk, who shook his head like Sam was nuts—jumping out without a parachute.

Sam gave a thumbs-up, smiled, looked out the doorway and jumped.

Wind pummeled Sam's face. He spread out his arms and changed his Stealth Suit to the same kind of BASE-jumping wing-suit he'd created at the Eiffel Tower.

In Paris, I had Zara hanging on and we still managed to glide down and land on a moving bus.

I've just got to get me down to the ground this time—should be a piece of cake.

Looking over his shoulder, he saw Henk peeling away. Now he just had to fulfill his part of the plan and create a good diversion at the other edge of the no-fly zone.

Sam figured he was gliding down through five thousand feet when he started panicking.

Not because of the height, but because of the flash he spotted at ground level.

The plume of a missile came streaking up into the sky, clearly homing in on him.

What!?

Sam closed his arms and legs, making himself smaller and more streamlined. With minimal wind resistance, he was now falling like a bullet, the air pounding against his face and shoulders.

The missile was nearing.

Three seconds.

Wait for it . . .

Two.

Sam threw open his arms and legs and his fall immediately slowed.

One—

WHOOSH!

The missile flashed by, the heat of its rocket engine searing him.

That was close!

He was surprised he'd been a big enough target to lock on to.

Sam looked over his shoulder. The missile was turning in a big, wide arc through the air and heading straight back.

For him.

It's picking up my body heat.

Sam, you fool!

He changed his Stealth Suit to invisible, knowing this would also dampen his heat signature. He looked over his shoulder again.

The missile was weaving left and right, then up and down, as though searching for a target that a moment ago had been right in front of it. It did a spiraling loop and curved away from him, headed away.

"All right! Take that!" Sam looked down at the ground below, now lit up with activity, but he felt confident that he was invisible to them. The guard dogs would be more of a problem but he had Henk doing something about that. Henk was going to the other side, where he'd land and make it on foot to the outer fence and dump the cooler of fish that he'd caught back at the islands. The stink would be enough for the dogs to get distracted.

Henk . . . oh no!

Sam looked to his right at the blinking of the helicopter's tail-light in the darkening sky.

And the red hot plume of the missile racing to catch it.

ALEX

Alex had a bump on his forehead the size of an egg and his left eye was swollen. The cool air that blew in from the sea was soothing. The painkillers he'd taken before he'd slept were still working.

He stumbled out onto the deck to find that the morning had brought with it a new world. The *Ra* had steamed through the night, full speed south and they had long ago passed into the Antarctic Circle.

The ice floes were big and jagged and dangerous looking, but the *Ra's* ice-breaking hull sliced a path through with ease. Alex was rugged up in a thick yellow snowsuit, standing on the frozen-over starboard deck. The *Ra* passed icebergs the size of houses, the sound of their heavy ice cracking and groaning in the quiet cold. Now they were navigating by apartment-building-size hunks of ice. The frozen continent was in sight.

"Never in my life did I think I'd see this," a deep voice said.

Alex turned to see Ahmed standing next to him, his breath fogging out over the sea.

"I didn't expect it to be so quiet," Alex said.

"Peaceful, but hostile," Ahmed said. "We are not meant to survive in such conditions."

"These suits will protect us," Alex said.

Ahmed nodded. "For a while. But you do not want to get separated from the group, stuck out on the ice, overnight."

"Because of frostbite?" Alex said. "I've read about it."

"Yes, very dangerous. Before you know it, you may have lost your fingers or toes."

"I'll be careful," Alex said.

"How is the head?"

"Still a bit sore."

"That was quite the tumble, for a moment we thought maybe that was it for you."

"*It*? Like I was a goner? Like . . . dead?"

"It was quite the bump on the head."

"You're telling me." Alex squinted against the gray sky, the clouds backlit from the sun that hid somewhere out of view.

They watched the scene in silence for a while. A massive ice wall, easily as tall as a twenty-story building, formed a cliff on one side as far as the eye could see. Every now and then huge pieces of frozen water would sheer off and cascade into the sea.

"What was in the safe?" Alex asked. "Did Hans find what he was looking for?"

"The log? Yes, but it's gone, destroyed by a water leak.

Nothing more than a pile of sludge."

"Where does that leave us?"

"We go by the old maps, hope that we can find the way. Or . . ."

"Or?" Alex prompted.

"If there's a Gear down there, we wait for the Dreamer to come along. If we search, even with the old maps, it will still be like finding a needle in a haystack."

"Do you really think that we'll find something down here?" Alex asked. "I mean, even with all the special equipment that we have, it's dangerous enough for *us* to be here, let alone some ancient seafaring people."

"Nonetheless, it seems there *was* something here, once," Ahmed said. "There are too many mentions through history and in ancient maps—including that carving of the coastline we found at Micronesia."

"Of a time before it was so iced over?"

"Mm-hmm," Ahmed said. "Of course, time seems to take much and leave little."

"I just don't see what could be in such a barren place."

"I've never stopped digging, Alex, and neither have others in my country. Egypt's hot deserts are just as barren as the cold deserts here," Ahmed said. "And what do you think they are digging for? Gold? No, dear Alex, it's *power*. It's power that keeps them digging."

"Power?" Alex said. "I don't understand."

"Power, fame. That's if they're legitimate archaeologists.

For treasure hunters, it's all about the money that will come from selling the artifacts on the black market. You see, that kind don't cherish what they find, they just want to find it before someone else. There are very few now, who, like me, dig for no other purpose than to preserve our history, to understand it, to learn from it."

"Then *why* are you working with Hans?" Alex said. "I thought you were working with Dr. Dark? I mean, doesn't Hans just want whatever is beyond the Dream Gate for himself?"

"Perhaps," Ahmed said. "But sometimes you need to work with others to achieve the outcome you desire."

"Make sure you're safe. And for the record, I still don't like it," Phoebe said. "Jack has a contact at one of the US bases down there. I'm going to give him your coordinates, should anything go wrong."

"Mom, I'll be fine."

"Alex, you don't understand," Phoebe said. "We've lost contact with Sam and Eva in Australia."

"When did you last hear from them?" he asked.

"Yesterday," Phoebe said. "They went there in disguise, and Lora and her team, all that are left of our Guardians, have gone to shut down Stella's operations."

"I'm sure they're OK," Alex said. "Sam always seems

to scrape through. And I sure hope that Lora catches up with Stella and she gets what's coming to her."

"Just worry about yourself and be safe, Alex."

Alex looked at the bright-orange submersible and swallowed hard. It had only five mechanical arms now, the missing appendage now sunk within the U-boat. The *Osiris* was in the water next to the *Ra*, ready to dive below the ice. The pilots were aboard, as was Ahmed, and all of their equipment. A German Guardian was in the spare seat.

"It's safer this way," Hans said to Alex. "I know it probably doesn't seem like it, but it is."

"I understand," Alex said. "This way we can travel under the ice for a few miles."

"Which I would rather do than scale the cliff and make it across the ice on skis," Hans said.

Alex looked up at the imposing white cliff face. "I still don't understand how we can go under the ice. I thought that more of the ice was under the water than above it."

"Technically, we'll be going *through* it," Hans said. "Warmer water has carved tunnels through the ice, big enough for vehicles to go through."

"Well, that makes more sense, I guess."

"And just like lava tubes on land, these tubes run for vast distances and will lead us to the heat source, which is a thermal lake in a cave system ten miles inland."

Thermal lake? This is starting to sound like my dream.

"—in the heated water from volcanic action," Hans was saying. "From satellite imagery penetrating the ice, the water temperature at the lake is only about ten degrees, because it's such a vast system. But some thermal lakes are much, much hotter than that—boiling, in fact, so you must be careful. We'll prep you on safety on the way in."

"And that old U-boat made this trip through the ice tubes?"

"Oh no, not at all," Hans said. "The ice is always changing and that submarine was too big. No, they made it overland, over the period of a week or more, but when they found the site, and the thermal lake and the tubes leading out, they floated markers in the water—and they all ended up at sea."

"So it's a shortcut!" Alex realized.

"Precisely."

"We're ready!" Karl called from inside the *Osiris*.

"No time like the present," Hans said.

For the second time in two days, Alex climbed aboard the *Osiris*. This time, he vowed, he'd keep his harness on and his head in one piece.

The journey through the ice tunnel took just over half an hour. At a depth of one hundred feet, the smooth white walls made for easy navigation. The two forward claw arms were extended out and at opposing angles, so as to be a first line of defense should an outcrop of ice block their way. So far it had been clear. They had made swift progress, buoyed by a steady current.

"We are coming up to the lake," Hans announced.

Alex, seated next to Ahmed again, watched on their monitors. The view from the forward cameras showed the tunnel disappearing—and a new world emerging.

They were in an enormous space, completely black but for a shimmer above where the water surface met the air pocket and the reflection waved back at them.

"Depth is two hundred sixty feet," Karl noted. "The surface of the water is approximately thirty feet above us. And according to the GPS, the ice cap above is nearly one hundred sixty-five feet thick. The lake stretches out from here nearly three miles in each direction."

"Take us to the hot spot," Hans said.

"Yes, sir."

"What's that?" Alex said.

"There are thermal vents to the south," Hans explained, reading off coordinates on his own GPS monitor. "They lead to the surface and near where we have to go."

"You seem pretty sure of that," Alex said. His monitor showed nothing but the reflection of their lights on the surface above as the tiny *Osiris* powered along in the subterranean lake.

"We managed to piece together enough of my grandfather's map to put us within a five-mile search grid on the coastal side of the mountain range."

"I thought all you found in the U-boat's safe was sludge?"

Hans passed over his tablet—it showed an image of a hand drawn map, pieced together from tiny fragments, all photographed or scanned.

"My tech guys worked through the night to get it that far," Hans said. "And they'll update us in the field should they get it more complete. But in the meantime, we go on."

"Perhaps Alex and I should have stayed aboard the *Ra*, until you had a team scout ahead," Ahmed said. "We are not trained adventurers."

"Nonsense!" Hans said with a smile. "You're going to be naturals!"

SAM

The missile was headed straight for Henk.

The helicopter was outside the restricted area and therefore not a legitimate threat or target, but the missile didn't know that. It had been fired at Sam, who'd then disappeared from its view, so it had gone searching for a new heat signature.

Any heat signature.

The red-hot engines of the helicopter were a prime target.

"Henk, look out!" Sam shouted helplessly into the air.

He watched as the missile flashed toward the aircraft at phenomenal speed, eating up the distance too fast. Henk had no chance—

KLAP-BOOM!

The missile exploded in an earsplitting bang and a huge flash of red flames.

Sam closed his eyes for a second and thought the worst, guilt immediately gripping him.

I brought him into this.

When Sam opened his eyes, he saw the helicopter still flying. He whooped with joy.

The controllers must have detonated it when it flew out of their restricted airspace!

Sam was still celebrating when he looked back at the ground below him.

"Oh no!"

He was coming in to land too fast.

Way too fast.

Moments after he changed his Suit to maximum padding, Sam hit hard on the dusty red earth, belly first. He skipped like a stone across water.

He may have been invisible, but he was kicking up clouds of dust with every bounce and he didn't seem to be slowing as he headed for the gatehouse and the boom gate across the road.

"Oh no!"

Sam brought his arms and legs into a ball and willed his Stealth Suit to protect him.

KLANG!

He got to his feet, stumbling around, the sound of bells ringing in his head. He checked his arms and legs, feeling for any injuries. As he looked up, he saw a Sam-size dent in the side of the gatehouse.

But I'm OK, I'm OK!

Sam deflated the Suit as the guard, who Sam had seen in his dream, came out of the hut, frantically looking around.

His dog was there too.

So much for a silent infiltration. But there's no time to do things any other way, no time to sit and wait until the alarm dies down.

Sam pulled his dart gun.

"Sorry, guys," he whispered, and the guard spooked as he looked from the huge dint in the side of his booth to— nothing. Sam was still invisible when he fired.

The guard fell instantly, unconscious.

The dog snarled and lunged forward.

Sam fired again.

The dog yelped as it fell to the ground, motionless.

Sam checked the dog, worried that the dart might be too powerful. But patting its side, he knew he didn't have to worry. This beast was practically the size and weight of a grown man anyway and it was now sound asleep.

Sam got to his feet, taking the guard's ID pass. "Hang on, Eva," he said, "I'm coming."

Sam crept out of the bullet train at the terminal and made his way to the underground cavern and lake. As he crossed over towards the bridge, two men suddenly appeared from around a corner.

Not the base security guys in their uniforms.

Agents.

Stella's rogue Agents.

But they can't see me.

Sam dropped the first guy with a kick to the knee and a jujitsu throw to the floor.

The other Agent spun around, looking for their attacker, realizing it must be someone in a Stealth Suit. He reacted by switching his own Suit to blend into the environment, but Sam already had a fix on him.

WHACK!

Sam darted the Agent in the back. The Agent slumped forward. Sam took the dart gun from the unconscious Agent. He now had a gun in each hand. It was different from the one he'd been given weeks ago by Tobias—this one had a longer barrel and held a larger clip of darts.

Sam headed across the bridge. On the far side, he could see the moving glow of flashlights.

Stella and Eva, he was sure.

EVA

"OK," Eva said. "OK!"

"Yes?" Stella sneered.

"I'll tell you," Eva said. "I'll tell you everything."

"Everything?" Stella said. "All I want to know is where the Gear is. So tell. Ticktock. Your friends are walking into a turkey shoot."

"Tell them to stand down."

"Excuse me?" Stella said, incredulous.

"Tell your Agents there at Chernobyl to stand down," Eva said. "Tell them to put down their weapons and walk away. Tell them that and I'll tell you where this Gear is. You win this round, and no one gets hurt."

Stella leaned in close, her sneer looming large as Eva squirmed away from her. "This round?" she spat. "You think this is a game, little girl? You need to wake up and see who's really in control here."

She strode back to the console and picked up a headset. "Attention all units," she said, turning back to look at Eva, "fire at will."

XAVIER

Xavier walked slowly alongside Lora. They were now behind the huge antenna structure and still had no more idea as to where an enemy might be lying in wait.

He could tell that Lora was wary.

If she's spooked, that's not good.

"Can you see anything?" he whispered.

"No."

"That's good, right?"

"I don't think so," Lora said.

She stopped, crouched down to the ground.

Xavier crouched next to her.

"Look," she said, pointing at the soft earth that covered the paving stones beneath their feet. "What do you see?"

"Footprints."

"Yep. Combat boots, lots of them." Lora drew her dart gun. "And they don't belong to our Guardians."

"They don't?"

"Nope." Lora looked around, worried now.

"How do you know?"

"I know," Lora said.

"So what do we—" Xavier said, interrupted by the earth-shattering sound of gunfire, right above them, breaking the silence into a million pieces.

"Get down!" Lora yelled, grabbing her mic. "Road team, report in!"

No reply. The shots kept coming, now shouts could be heard above the bullets raining down around them. Lora grabbed Xavier by his bulletproof vest and pulled him to a pillar next to the windows.

"Don't move," she whispered. "Road team, report."

There was nothing—just static.

"All teams, do you copy?"

More static.

Lora gripped her dart pistol in both hands. "Whoever it is, they're playing for keeps."

"Stella?" Xavier whispered back, checking his weapon, his heart thudding in his chest.

"Follow me," Lora said, "and keep it quiet."

They ran quickly and quietly to the control room of the antenna and carefully approached the windows, the glass long ago—many years ago—broken and gone.

The Guardians were there.

But they were all lying motionless. Bullets littered the ground.

Lora cursed and pulled Xavier away from the windows,

but not before he'd caught a glimpse.

All the men and women who'd just been with us—now all dead.

Xavier could feel his panic rising as he watched Lora pull out a gun. Her hands shook, ever so slightly, but her face was resolute.

"They might think they got everyone," Lora said, "but we've got to stay calm. I'll get you out of this, I promise."

"How about—wait, can you hear something?" Xavier said.

It was the sound of a car speeding down the road. It was a massive SUV with blacked-out windows.

It's practically a tank!

And it was definitely not their designated pickup vehicle.

Lora and Xavier took aim with their dart guns.

The vehicle stopped in front of them and the driver's window slid down noiselessly.

Xavier did a double take.

"Dad?"

"Xavier, get in. We have to go!" Dr. Dark said.

Lora and Xavier needed no second invitation. They raced out to the car and it tore away, a spray of bullets landing on the roof as the car flew down the deserted road.

Lora was already on her phone frantically relaying the attack to Jedi, getting him to call in the local authorities.

"Look, behind us!" Dr. Dark called.

Xavier and Lora looked out the rear window of the car.

Dozens of Agents appeared out of nowhere, converging fast in the middle of the road, racing to catch them.

We made it.

But we're the only ones left now.

34

EVA

"**Y**ou're a monster!" Eva screamed, hot tears of anguish and defiance streaming down her face.

Stella turned from Eva to the screen, looking at the carnage at Chernobyl and simply shrugged.

Eva strained against her bindings. Her wrists were almost free. If she could get loose, and get Stella close enough, and off guard, she could . . .

What? What could I do?

Something. Anything!

"It's done," Stella said, pointing at the screen. "You lose, as you always will. And ultimately I will get what I want. So don't make me torture you, just give it to me now and maybe you can spare yourself some pain."

Eva watched as dozens of Agents calmly got into their vehicles and began to drive away. The camera view changed again and she winced to see the dozens of bodies lying in the dirt, lifeless and abandoned.

"Now you know what I'm prepared to do," Stella said. "Tell me where the next Gear is. I'm done talking to you."

SAM

SMASH!

The Agent took the blow and turned with it, throwing Sam across the floor and sending him smashing into a vending machine that started spewing out chocolate bars.

His Stealth Suit flickered and then stayed on, visible for all to see. Sam looked down to find he was wearing a bright-pink Hawaiian shirt and a kilt with yellow-and-blue tartan.

"Great time to malfunction," Sam muttered under his breath.

On his back, Sam looked up as the Agent neared for another attack. He'd been taken completely by surprise. An Agent had come silently around a blind corner and sprung into action with lightning speed. They were in the recreation area just off the rear entrance to the vault, plastic tables and chairs scattering as they fought.

Right now, Sam had an ever growing pile of out-of-date chocolate bars raining down on his chest.

And the Agent was a couple of paces away and nearing fast.

Sam threw a handful of chocolate bars at the Agent's face, causing him to flinch, and he kept throwing, a peanut bar catching the guy in the eye.

"Arghh!" The Agent was momentarily blinded.

Sam used the distraction to spin around on the ground, tripping the Agent.

CRACK!

The big guy landed hard on the floor and hit his head, out cold.

"Man," Sam said, standing up and brushing himself off, picking up his dart gun and shooting the Agent in the leg to be sure that he remained out of it for a while longer. "Never," he said, eating a chocolate bar as he walked away, "sneak up on a hungry teenager."

EVA

"I don't believe you," Stella said.

"It's true!" Eva replied, almost free of the binds behind her back.

"You're telling me that you took the Gear from the vault," Stella said, "and for some reason it's hidden just through this door?"

"Yes." Eva felt her wrist slipping free and she had a sudden flush of adrenaline as she imagined what she had to do next.

I gotta rush Stella as soon as she turns her back to go through the door towards the vault. It's my only chance.

"If you're lying," Stella said, her hand on the door handle. "You know there will be consequences . . ."

SAM

Sam ran hard at the door marked VAULT and hit it with every bit of force that he had.

Unlike the previous door he'd broken down, this one seemed to give right away. In fact, it crashed open so easily and so fast that it was like it was being opened from the other side.

"Sam!"

"Eva?" Sam said, worried for a moment that he'd knocked her to the ground.

He hadn't.

Eva stood before him.

Sam looked down.

Stella was there, dazed, and looked up at him with shock and then anger in her eyes.

WHACK!

Stella fired at Sam, and Sam dived but was too late— the dart hit him in the face, cracking the lens of his glasses and stuck there, half an inch from his eyeball.

"Not," Sam said, ditching the smashed glasses, "cool."

WHACK!

Sam fired point-blank, the dart hitting Stella squarely in the shoulder. Her eyes rolled back in her head as she slumped against the ground.

"Nice shot!" Eva said.

"I should have gone for the head," Sam grimaced.

"What took you so long?" Eva asked, untying her other wrist.

"Did a bit of sightseeing," Sam said. "You got the Gear?"

"Got it," Eva said, bending down to take her necklace back from Stella. She showed Sam the tiny little Gear that hung next to her dream catcher charm. "Stella had it right in her hand and didn't even see it."

"How'd you get the code to the vault?" Sam asked.

"The dream—I saw it," Eva said, smiling. "Well, it was probably *my* dream, right?"

"The code was 'thirteen,' as numbered letters, right?"

"With X equaling one," Eva nodded. "But Sam, there's something you should know, I saw Stella's Agents in—"

"Not now," Sam interrupted. "Tell me everything once we're out of here."

"You're right, of course, let's go."

They turned to go back and stopped—

There was a new presence there.

Solaris.

ALEX

"If we're naturals at this," Alex said to himself, trudging slowly across the snow, "I'd hate to see an amateur out of his depth."

He was third in the line, all of them linked by ropes. The Guardian in the lead, dressed in a red snowsuit, was a mountaineer who'd summited the world's seven tallest peaks. Then there was Hans, Alex, and lastly, poor old Ahmed. Three matching yellow snowsuits in a row.

All four of them carried backpacks full of survival gear, and fifteen feet of red rope was strung between each of them, tied onto climbing harnesses around their waists.

Alex looked back over his shoulder and saw Ahmed, his hooded head down, shuffling miserably. Behind him, steam rose from the vent tube they'd been winched up from, the winch and beacon still there for their return leg.

"We're *so* not trained for this," Alex said under his breath. He looked ahead and kept on trudging. Hans was in front of him, the Guardian at the front, GPS unit in hand. About two hours by foot, he'd said.

This is going to be a long day.

They stopped forty-five minutes in, using the cover of a rocky outcrop against the strengthening wind to have a hot drink. A gas-bottle-fed campfire heated water and tea and sugar was added. Lots of sugar, to keep their energy up. They'd eaten granola bars in silence, the expedition leader radioing back and smiling, clearly in his element. Then they set off again.

"Have to race the weather!" the Guardian said before pulling up his balaclava to cover his nose and face, pulling down his goggles. "Follow me—let's see if we can make it another forty-five minutes before the next break."

The weather beat them to it.

Alex was walking diagonally into the wind, mimicking those ahead of him, to stay on his feet.

Snow and ice crystals blew in hard, but there was nowhere to shelter.

Underfoot, the ground had changed from snow powder to hard ice, deep fissures in places, which they had to skirt around. Thirty minutes in and Alex was so tired he could hardly move his legs. Worse, Ahmed had almost stopped, the archaeologist practically being dragged along by the rope connecting the four of them together. Up ahead, Hans and the Guardian stopped. Soon the four of them huddled together, face-to-face against the increasing wind and biting cold.

"Another three hundred feet!" the Guardian said against the howl of the wind. "The fissures in the ground are getting bigger. We can find one to shelter in until this passes over!"

"OK!" Hans said.

"One step at a time, then tug on the rope and take another!" the Guardian yelled. "And we continue on like that, OK?"

The four of them gave the thumbs-up and set off, headfirst into the crosswind.

The snow was now so thick in the air that it was a full-blown blizzard. Visibility had dropped to the point where Alex could only see the red rope connecting them and not the figures of Hans and Ahmed to his immediate front and back. They'd step, tug the rope, he'd step, tug the rope . . .

"Arghh!" Alex was being dragged forward. He knew instantly what had happened—the Guardian had slipped down a fissure, his weight threatening to drag them all down with him.

Alex dug in his heels, the long steel teeth of the crampons gouging through the hard ice.

Ahmed didn't stop behind him. He was pulled off his feet and slid past Alex like a bowling ball tossed down a well-polished lane.

Alex was now being pulled forward by three grown men, the ropes at his waist dragging him down.

He was pulled to the ground and onto his side, sliding headfirst towards the others, to what he imagined was a bottomless crevasse. Without a moment to spare, Alex drew the knife from the sheath on his pack and cut both the ropes.

There was only snow and ice—desolate, blinding.

It had been an hour since he'd last seen the others, and he'd skirted the crevasse, one slow step at a time, calling out, hopeful.

Then, the weather cleared. The blizzard passed. The dull gray sky was replaced by an ice-cold blue, the sun low on the horizon.

Must find shelter.

Who's going to find me?

I'm going to die out here.

"No, not like this!" Alex screamed at the sky. "You hear me? I have a destiny to live out!"

The eerie silence closed in around him.

With nothing more than the pack on his back, and no other choice, Alex trudged on. Finally he made the top of the ridge. He cleared the ice from his goggles.

There was a valley—rocky, with hardly any snow,

and—water. A lake in the middle and all around it, orange and green moss in hardy clumps. Steam rose from the water.

It's warm. Must be geothermal.

The heat of lava flowing near the surface heats the ground keeping the lake liquid. For thousands of years, it would have been an oasis, a refuge for anyone down here.

The other side of the ridge was a steady decline of loose gravel that looked like it would be hard going.

Not exactly a tropical oasis.

But it was the best hope he'd had in over an hour.

Is this the only place like this here? No, it can't be. Not on a huge continent like Antarctica.

He took a couple of small steps to start his descent—

"Arghh!"

The wind gusted and blew him over, tumbling him down the mountainside. Alex felt like he was inside a washing machine—filled with gravel. He pulled his arms in over his face, and brought his knees to his chest, forming a ball and rocketing down. Covered in all the snow gear, he didn't feel anything until . . .

CRASH!

Alex hit the bottom of the valley and slid. He shot out his hands and feet to slow the slide but it was useless. He was on the orange-green mossy lichen, and it was wet and slippery, and he was now sliding facedown, headfirst, towards the water pool.

The *steaming* water pool.

Oh boy . . .

Alex pushed his toes into the moss. His boots bit hard, slowing him.

CLINK!

The crampons detached against the strain.

In five seconds he'd hit the water.

I'll be a boiled lobster in five seconds!

Alex used every bit of strength he had left to shift his weight, pushing down with his heels while he shoved himself upright with his arms. He turned his toes inwards, forming a V-shape, just like he'd learned to do on skis as a boy.

It's working—I'm slowing down!

Alex put all his weight forward to the outer edges of his boots, and they bit into the fine sandy gravel under the moss. The final three feet of ground before the water was barren.

Too hot for anything to grow.

He hit that and instantly his boots gained traction, gouging two troughs until . . .

He stopped.

The water lapped at the front of his boots. The pool was steaming and bubbling.

Not a friendly warm bath-type of pool, then. Definitely more the lobster type.

"Wow, that was close."

Then he smelled it. A sickly, sweet smell, like burning plastic or rubber.

"Ow!"

Alex stepped away from the water's edge as he saw the soles of his boots melting on the hot gravel. Up and down the valley it seemed much the same as this, the hot lake in the middle, the growth all around it.

There were a few places down the valley where the water was broken up by larger rocks that formed bridges, and Alex took one of these to the other side. This side grew steeper, faster, and the plant growth was minimal, in some places sparse enough for him to jump over and walk on the frozen rocks.

To his side, up the steep rock wall towards another ridge, were deep, dark fissures.

Alex checked the time.

"I should shelter for the night," he said to himself. He walked along the fissures, looking for one that might be deep enough to fit in.

Not that there is night here. So weird having daylight all the time. But my body's saying it's time to sleep.

The evening light hit the white snow-covered top of the opposite ridge, impossibly bright even at this hour.

The next place I find that's big enough, I'm squeezing in.

He rounded a large rocky outcrop. The water here was at its widest, bubbling and steaming. He kept against the rock wall, using his gloved hands to find a way forward. Where the rocks met at another outcrop, there was an opening. He felt around it—it was just big enough. He pushed himself inside. The rock face on his back and front was tight against the puffy snowsuit. He stopped, relaxed.

Not large enough to lie down, but I can sit and sleep, my back against the rock wall.

He tried to wriggle out to check his supplies before settling in and stopped.

He realized his other arm, deeper into the space, was moving freely. It was as though it had passed the tightest spot between the rocks and found a wider space beyond. He backed out, took a glow stick from a pouch on his arm and snapped it, shaking it until it came to life.

He undid the top half of his snowsuit and pushed it down past his waist, forcing his way back into the space. With the fluorescent yellow light, he could see a few feet around him. He pushed on through the closest points between the rock walls and into . . .

"Wow—it's some kind of natural cave," Alex murmured in surprise.

A tiny pool of heated water in the middle made the cave warm too.

Awesome.

I might be marooned in Antarctica, but at least I'm not going to die of hypothermia.

Although starvation is still going to be a problem. Huh.

Alex noticed something else as he shuffled farther in.

The floor's smooth, and the walls. They'd been carved into the rock.

This is no natural cave.

SAM

A jet of fire flashed to the right of them and splattered against the water.

"Turn invisible!" Eva said to Sam as they ran across the bridge.

"I can't!" Sam said, running next to her. "Suit's broken!"

"That explains the kilt!"

WHOOSH!

Another jet of fire, this one hitting the ground at the back of their heels.

"Wait!" Sam said and stopped.

Eva skidded to a stop a few paces ahead.

Sam turned around.

Solaris' black-clad figure, his form shimmering, was some hundred feet back on the bridge.

Sam looked out over the lake, the water rushing below. The underground structure had been carved into the rock from the natural salt cavern that had come into being over millions of years. To the side of the vault platform, giant concrete water tanks, each the size of a suburban house, formed a wall.

Next to them were the generator turbines that powered the base. And between those spinning turbines and the water storage tanks was a huge gas turbine generator.

"Give me the Gear," Solaris said through his rasping mask. "You've got nowhere to go."

Sam took out the flare gun that Henk had given him, raised it and fired.

Solaris laughed as the round flew up into the air far over his head.

"You little fool," Solaris said. "You are a worse shot than I ever imagined, Sam."

"Am I?" Sam said.

Solaris was silent, then looked over his shoulder.

Just in time to see the flare arcing through the air. Its bright-white and orange phosphorous core, burning at a thousand degrees, was curving down.

Towards the generator.

Sam turned and grabbed Eva's arm and they ran for the exit.

He didn't need to see the impact.

He heard it. And felt it.

KLAP-BOOM!

The force of the explosion sent a shockwave of air rushing over them as they ran.

A new sound followed.

Sam looked over his shoulder.

The water tank closest to the gas tanks shattered—

and began a chain reaction as the pressure was suddenly released and the broken concrete from one tank slammed out at its neighbor, each tank doing the same as the weight of the water inside broke through the cracks.

BOOM, BOOM, BOOM, BOOM!

A wall of water came rushing behind Sam and Eva as they ran across the bridge.

Sam remembered Alex's dream—and his warning.

A tsunami.

EVA

"I always wanted to see Australia," Eva said, swatting away some flies.

"Me too," Sam said.

They'd hidden among some rocks, a few miles west of the government installation and now dawn had broken. Neither had slept. Instead, they'd talked in hushed tones about what they'd seen and heard since they were last together. They waited quietly, listening for any guards who might be searching for them. Around them there was only the vast empty landscape of desert scrub.

"Hey, you haven't told me," Eva said. "What'd you find on that island up north?"

"A cool local guy named Malcolm. He'd seen us in his dreams."

"He's a Dreamer too?" Eva asked. "Wait. I saw him in *my* dream, when I first saw all this."

"Nice. He showed me a sacred place," Sam said. "There was a tunnel that led under the rock of the island, to a sacred cavern."

"What was in there?" Eva asked.

"It was a crystal chamber, like the one I saw in Japan with Issey. A chamber used to read dream waves via the energy they produce. The early Australians must have known about it too and they kept it a secret until the time was right."

"What time?"

"Our time—the time of the last 13. A time when people would know what to do with it. I mean, what would they say to the world? That they found a machine buried deep under a rock in the middle of an island, built tens of thousands of years before we could even imagine machines like that?"

"Machines? You're saying this crystal chamber was a machine?"

"In a sense. It's a dream machine."

"And how does it work?" Eva asked.

"We turn it on, it affects the Dreamspace. Malcolm said there was a big room like it under Uluru, that when activated will start up a new Dreamtime on this continent. It'll help transform the world. I think that's what we're getting towards, at the end of all this."

"Do you think there's another machine at the Dream Gate?"

"I think that whatever it is, it'll lead to answers, about who built these chambers, how they built them, for what purpose, and why they've been forgotten all through time but for a few Dreamers."

"So we have to go in there, and switch this machine on?"

"That was my dream."

"But we have the next Gear, and I think that's what really matters now," Eva said, shielding her eyes from the sun. "We can come back later."

Sam had a pained look as he looked around the landscape.

"We're splitting up again," Eva said. "Aren't we?"

Sam nodded.

"You want to stay, to see what this machine will do?"

"I have to."

"Because some old guy told you to?"

"No, because I'm following my dream," Sam said. He took Eva's hands in his. She held back tears. "You go back to the Academy—first flight you can. You have your passport, plenty of money. Get that Gear back to London. Stay there, with the others."

"And you?"

"I'll be fine."

A little mob of rock wallabies bounced by them, making Eva laugh.

I can't help but think we should stay together.

"I'm sick of losing people I care about," she said.

"You're not losing me," Sam said with a smile. "Besides, if I don't do this, who knows what will happen?"

"Who knows what will happen if you *do?* This machine has been abandoned all this time for a reason."

Sam hugged Eva and then pointed to a dirt track.

"About five miles. You take the last of the water. Find a tour group and join them, they'll take you back to Alice Springs, and from there you can get home."

"Home . . ."

"The Academy. That's your home now."

"And where's yours, Sam?"

Sam looked at the Rock, the pull of the place, the specialness, tugging at him, calling him.

Can't he just stay with me, by my side, for these final couple of steps of the race?

"Right now, it's here," he said, "until I dream otherwise."

Suddenly the sound of a helicopter broke the still morning air.

Sam looked up and saw a familiar shape.

"It's Henk!" Sam said. "The guy that flew me in."

The helicopter spotted them and touched down. They could see that Henk was not alone.

Jabari was with him. He got out and ran over to them.

"I'm so glad you two are OK!" he said.

Eva hugged him.

"You got the Gear?" he asked.

"Here," Eva said, showing him the tiny double-disk Gear around her neck.

"I've got news," Jabari said. "Lora and Xavier are alive— they got out with Dr. Dark. They even managed to blow the Chernobyl-2 site. The charges were laid just in time . . ."

"So it's offline?" Sam asked.

"Offline forever," Jabari said.

"What did you mean 'just in time'?" Eva asked.

"There were . . . casualties," Jabari said. "I—I may be one of only a few of my kind left now."

"No!" Eva gasped. "I'm so sorry."

"And there is more bad news, I'm afraid," Jabari added.

"What is it?" Sam asked.

"It's Alex," Jabari said, his voice grave. "We've lost him. Last we heard, he was hiking with Hans. But a few hours ago, a severe snowstorm hit Antarctica and now we can't reach him."

"How . . ." Eva's voice trailed off—but not because she'd lost her train of thought, but because she was falling to the ground. She reached up and touched the dart sticking in her neck.

In her last moments, she saw movement flickering in the heat haze—several figures appeared out of nowhere, their Stealth Suits becoming visible again. She turned her head just in time to see Sam and Jabari collapsing under a hailstorm of darts.